THE MYSTERY OF RUBY'S STILETTO

ROSE DONOVAN

Moon Snail Press

MORE RUBY DOVE MYSTERIES

Join my reader group! Details can be found at the end of *The Mystery of Ruby's Stiletto.*

Cast of Characters at Villa Sprezzatura

Ruby Dove – Student of chemistry at Oxford, fashion designer and amateur spy-sleuth. Thrilled by Renzo Carnevali's shoe designs.

Fina Aubrey-Havelock – Student of history at Oxford, assistant seamstress to Ruby and her best friend. Thrilled to travel to Sardinia.

Ruggero Bianchi – Valet-cum-butler with a knuckle-cracking habit. Out of place at the Villa Sprezzatura.

Renzo Carnevali – Famous Italian shoe designer. Adriana's brother. Host and hypochondriac.

Fabrizio De Sio – Taciturn – or secretive – cook who loves to swim.

Zenash Araya Ezana – Famous writer exiled from Addis Ababa. A restless artist.

Irene Finlay – London art critic and close friend of Adriana. Spotter of forgeries.

Idris Maghur – Exiled architect from Tripoli with a love of history.

Adriana Orso – Sister of Renzo. Painter extraordinaire who loves artistic clothing.

Nefeli Papas – Greek accountant by day. Enjoys owning, but not wearing, the latest fashions.

Silvio Rametti – Renzo's private doctor from London with an impressive track record. And even more impressive hair.

Gina Scarpa – Dancer and *lettore* with a jealous streak. Wife of Nicola.

Nicola Scarpa – Sardinian shoemaker and nationalist. Husband of Gina.

Carlotta Visconti – Opera singer, lover of impossibly high heels and unfortunate wife of leather magnate Vito Visconti. Renzo's guest of honour.

Divo and Diva – Crafty cats with a knack for causing accidents.

Some characters are absent from the list to avoid story spoilers.

1
———

"What a shame he'll spoil our lovely breakfast," said Ruby as she peered at the small rectangular calling card.

Fina shielded her eyes as she watched the approaching figure. The light from the sparkling Mediterranean behind him created only a silhouette, but she would recognise that loping gait anywhere. Her hunk of bread with pecorino cheese buried deep in its crusty folds fell onto her plate. Quickly wiping her fingers on her napkin, she then gripped the sides of her chair and inhaled the calming scent of eucalyptus.

It was James Matua. Breathe, Fina, breathe. Smile. Be casual.

She leant over to Ruby across the table, nearly plunging her hair into the remainders on her plate. "What should we say to James? How will he explain the miraculous coincidence of us all being in Sardinia at the same time?"

"He must have followed us from Oxford. The British government – or other interests – must have sent him," Ruby said, pausing. "Don't worry – we have a perfectly legitimate reason to be here. He's the one who will have to explain himself." She stiffened her back as if her own words offered physical support. "But this means we'll need to take the earlier ferry to Agrodolce."

Leaning back in her chair, Fina tried to appear nonchalant and unbothered by this complete surprise. Smiling as she surveyed the sea, she tilted her nose and inhaled as if to make a show of enjoying the salty air. She pulled her light wrap around her shoulders. November in Sardinia was still glorious, though an occasional cool breeze clashed with her idea of the sun-drenched island.

She craned her neck to the side and watched James pad toward them, escorted by a waiter. His longish hair flopped over his eyes in the way of an eternal schoolboy. His new light-grey suit struck a discordant note with his boyish face and gait. The beautiful cut indicated the suit must be from Milan. He gave them a squinting smile, remedied only by sunglasses drawn from his breast pocket.

James halted at their table, as awkwardly as a guest who has arrived at a dinner party empty-handed. He stuck out a hand toward Ruby. "Ruby and Fina! I say, it's quite a coincidence, what?" he said as Ruby half rose from her seat to give him a handshake.

She slid back into her seat and smoothed her hair. "What a pleasant surprise. It's a small world as they say, isn't it?" said Ruby. The left corner of her mouth lifted ever so slightly into a smile–smirk.

Fina swore Ruby was enjoying James' discomfort. She looked so completely at ease as Fina shook James' hand.

"What are you doing here and how the deuce did you find us?" asked Fina.

"I forgot you're not one for beating around the bush, are you?" he said with a sly grin. The man was playing for time, though he ought to have got his story straight before he arrived on the terrace. His satchel dropped to the floor. He bent over and scooped it up slowly.

Fina blinked. "I am one to come straight to the point."

He gave out a nervous chuckle and rubbed his hands together. "Well, I'm here for the European tennis championships. They'll be held in a few days' time in Cagliari, so I decided to play tourist. I hired a car to drive all over this spectacular island," he said, giving a little wave around their surroundings as if to illustrate.

"I didn't know you played tennis," said Ruby. "Isn't it a little late in the season for a tennis championship?"

"I grew up playing tennis in New Zealand," he replied. "I've found it difficult to combine my studies with sport but I cannot seem to give it up."

"You must be a smashing player if you're in a European championship," said Fina drily.

Responding with sincerity in his voice, he said, "I'm fortunate to have a natural talent for it."

Odd. James was forever dropping things. She didn't consider him to be particularly skilled at hand-eye coordination.

He cleared his throat. "It is an unusual time of year for a tennis competition. But we've had a few setbacks given the political situation in Italy at the moment. The organisers didn't want Mussolini to use the championship as his own photo opportunity. Their solution was to move it to Sardinia."

Plausible story. Even if it was a bit of a stretch.

"How did you find us?" asked Ruby.

"Oh, that," he said with a sheepish grin. "I'll admit I spotted you two in the street yesterday. You were walking with your backs toward me, so I couldn't wave at you. I watched you enter the hotel. It was late last night, so I thought I'd look you up in the morning," he said, adjusting his sunglasses and flopping his head back so his hair slid back from his eyes. "It's quite a rum coincidence. What are you two doing here? It's an odd time of year to travel to Italy."

Ruby puckered her lips. "Renzo Carnevali, the shoe designer, invited us to his villa on the island of Agrodolce. You can see it in the distance," she said, pointing out to sea. When Fina squinted at the island, she felt a little thrill zinging through her veins. "I met him in Paris. He has offered to mentor me – or, I ought to say, the two of us," she said, smiling at Fina, "and to introduce us to the world of shoemaking. I know plenty about clothes, but not about shoes."

Ruby swept her hand across the table which was covered in the detritus of breakfast. "I'm afraid we've already finished breakfast, though I'm sure they can bring you something if you're keen to join us."

He backed away almost imperceptibly from the table. "I say, that's awfully good of you. But I've already eaten. What are your plans for the day?"

Fina glanced at Ruby. Ruby rubbed her nose, a sure sign that she was about to be stingy with the truth. "We're visiting a famous shoemaker friend of Renzo's this morning. Then we're going to play tourists this afternoon. Would you like to join us?"

"Topping idea." His right hand quivered.

"Right. That's settled. We'll meet in the lobby at one o'clock."

"Right-o. I'll see you two later then," he said, loping off in the direction from which he had come.

Fina leant over and hissed, "What are you doing? Why are we giving him a chance to follow us?"

Ruby leant over. She was about to open her mouth when she snapped it shut like a goldfish. Her eyes widened. She whispered, "I don't believe it. She's here, in our hotel!"

2

———

A chattering group waltzed onto the terrace as if they were the opening act for a dance production in the West End. Clustered together, they moved as one unit, following the waiter's lead to the table nearest the sea.

Ruby leant over and whispered, "That's Zenash Araya Ezana!"

Fina held her breath, waiting for more.

Ruby looked exasperated. "You know, the writer in exile from Addis Ababa. She wrote *Pomegranates and Figs*. I'm not sure where she's living – I mean permanently – at the moment. She gave lectures in London for a time. Wendell met her in person. Now it's his turn to be jealous!"

Fina smiled at Ruby's excitement. Ruby was not competitive as a rule but when it came to her brother she transformed into a different person.

Ruby's eyes lit up. "I've remembered I have a copy of *Pomegranates and Figs* in my luggage upstairs. Do you think she would sign it for me?"

"I'm sure she would. Why don't you fetch it and I'll stay here, soaking up a bit more sun. And eavesdropping for juicy titbits from their table."

Ruby dashed across the terrace and then slowed to a trot as she entered the hotel.

Fina took a slice of orange from the table and began to chew its sweet insides. Sardinia would be a fabulous place to live, she thought absently. She tried not to stare at Zenash and company. Zenash wore a long, flowing yellow linen dress with a necklace with a cameo sort of pendant at the end. A delicate paper-thin pink flower peaked out from her hair when she turned to the left.

Next to her sat an extraordinarily handsome man with a quick smile in a longish brown linen shirt. He had a habit of folding his hands in his lap when speaking. They would sporadically fly up like birds from under the table and then would settle down as if they had closed their wings.

Rounding out the group was a woman in a forest green blouse and cream-coloured trousers. Her posture was remarkable for its consistency. Fina had noticed that most people, even those with exemplary posture, did tend to bend and change it as they engaged in conversation. The woman in the green blouse had a certain economy of movement. She took a bite of her toast, lowered it to the plate and still held it there, as if to preserve energy. Then she took another bite; a bite of exactly the same size.

Fina shook her head and awakened from her reverie. Her power of observation and photographic memory had come in handy during their previous cases in the Caribbean and home in England. It was her sleuthing moment of triumph when she had remembered every suspect's favourite cocktail on that fateful night.

She stretched back in her chair and gazed out over the

gorgeous sea, smiling at the memory of her sleuthing adventures with Ruby.

"Miss Ezana–" said the man.

"Please do call me Zenash. I much prefer it."

"Zenash, then. And you must call me Idris. Last I heard you were in London. Are you still living there?"

"I'm living in Paris, for the time being, but I'll return to London after leaving Sardinia. I don't seem to stay anywhere more than a few months. Not only do I get restless, but there's usually a political reason to move on."

Idris nodded in a knowing way. "I'm keen on returning to Tripoli – well, actually outside of Tripoli – but the political situation is too hot there. I'm living in London for now, but will most likely move to Barcelona soon. A city of marvellous architecture, so I'm not missing out on anything."

The woman in the green blouse queried, "Are you an architect, Mr Maghur?"

"Yes, Miss Papas. For my sins. I've tried other work but nothing ever takes. Or, I ought to say, nothing ever takes to me."

"Why is that, Mr Maghur?"

"Please do call me Idris. I am a Berber Jew, so I've had to build up my reputation enough in architecture circles to be taken seriously. It's hard for me to get a normal job," he sighed. Shifting in his seat, he said, "And you, Miss Papas?"

"I'm here because Mr Carnevali invited me," she replied. "I'm from Rhodes. I'm an accountant. I grew up in London but returned to Rhodes a few years ago. I have rheumatism so I moved to Rhodes for the warm climate and sea air. I also have plenty of family there."

"An accountant? How fascinating," said Zenash with sincerity. She paused, clearly waiting for an explanation.

Ruby returned, distracting Fina from the conversation. She leant over to Ruby, who was clutching a book in her hands as if it were the first thrilling day of primary school. "At least one of the group will join us on the island," whispered Fina.

"What?" hissed Ruby. "Is it Zenash?"

"I'm not sure, but it does give you an opening line of introduction," said Fina.

Ruby popped up and trundled over to the table.

"I'm so sorry to disturb you, but my friend Fina and I," she said, gesturing toward Fina, "couldn't help but overhear that one of you will join the weekend party at Mr Carnevali's island."

Zenash said, "Actually, all three of us will travel there this afternoon."

3

———

After Ruby and Fina introduced themselves and gushed about Zenash's books, a throat-clearing noise came from behind them.

Fina spied the same waiter who had escorted James onto the terrace earlier. He appeared apologetic. Or was it exasperated?

"A Mr Carnevali is here for you, Miss Aubrey-Havelock, and you, Miss Dove."

Ruby and Fina made their polite excuses and retreated to the cool interior of the Hotel Sardu. As her eyes adjusted to the dimness, Fina saw a small, wiry man with a broad face. His impressive salt and pepper hair was his defining feature. Though dressed in impeccable clothes, Fina's eyes focused on his sensational burgundy shoes. Absolute classics which still had an intense originality. And he exuded energy from every pore.

He bounded up to them. "Miss Dove. I am so pleased you accepted my invitation," he said, shaking Ruby's hand so fiercely Fina worried he might dislocate her arm. Not an ounce of fat on his wiry, graceful body. All lean muscle.

He spun his feet toward Fina. "And you must be Miss

Aubrey-Havelock. I've admired your beadwork on Ruby's latest creations. Exquisite."

Fina's face flashed oven-hot and then eased into a mellow glow of relaxed pride. "Why thank you, Mr Carnevali. That is praise I'll treasure from someone so talented," she said, giving a little unintentional bow.

He held his hand to his chest. "Please, no need to – how do you say? Butter me up. I have a swollen head already. Do call me Renzo."

"And now," he said, putting his hands on his hips, "shall we be off, ladies?"

As they strolled down Corso Umberto, Fina marvelled at the wooden barrels in the street, as wide as two or three people.

"What's in those barrels, Renzo?" she asked, tapping him on the shoulder after he extricated himself from embracing a passing friend.

"Those are full of wine!" he said, "and we shall have plenty of that this weekend."

They turned the corner from a dirt-covered street to one with cross-hatched stonework. A beautiful piazza opened up with children playing in one corner and old men sitting on benches in the other. Fina wiggled her nose as she caught a whiff of freshly baked bread and coffee. Flocks of swifts looped and dived in front of the wrought iron balconies.

"This is Piazza Regina Margherita. It is my favourite spot for an espresso," said Renzo, gesturing to the tables near the group of old men. Every few feet occasioned a new explanation of a house, a ruin, a street, a monument or a shop. Or a character who clapped Renzo on the back. It was clear from the twenty minutes it took them to travel just a few minutes' walk that everyone in Terranova Pausania knew Renzo.

"And here we are," he said, as he gestured toward a carved wooden sign above a dingy shopfront. The sign read "Scarpa", as if it were sufficient explanation. In this case, it was indeed enough. Ruby had told Fina that Nicola Scarpa's workshop was among the finest in Italy.

Renzo removed his sunglasses and waved them inside. A wall of leather and paint odours smacked Fina as she entered. She didn't find it an unpleasant smell in general, except it was almost unbearable at this level of intensity. With one woozy step after another, she followed Renzo and Ruby to the rear of the building. The small shopfront hid a spacious floor plan. She estimated the Scarpas employed at least twenty people. They worked at a rapid but unhurried pace. Everyone who glanced up from their tasks gave them a smile. Hearing a voice which sounded like a news announcer, Fina scanned the room for a Victrola or a radio. Seeing nothing, she looked elsewhere for the source of the headlines.

Her eyes rested on a petite woman perched on a tall stool in the middle of the shop. She held a newspaper in her hands and continued to read the newspaper aloud. Though her body was small, she had a robust pair of lungs. Despite being clad in the clothes of the workers around her, they somehow sat differently on her frame.

Renzo waved at the woman. She slid off the seat and bounced elegantly to the floor. She and Renzo gave each other obligatory side kisses and muttered a few words under their breath. She glided into what appeared to be an office.

"That is Gina Scarpa. The dancer. And wife of Nicola Scarpa," said Renzo. "A delightful woman," he said with enthusiasm.

"Why was she reading the newspaper out loud?" asked Fina.

"You must have *lettore* in England? Or perhaps they've fallen out of fashion," he said in response to the blank stares on their faces. "A *Lettore* reads the newspaper to workers as they work. It keeps them occupied and also keeps them educated about the politics of the day. We try to keep it quiet from the authorities. It's easier to do, since we're in Sardinia."

"Smashing idea," said Ruby. "Now you mention it, I have heard about this in the Caribbean," she paused. "But you said she's a dancer. Why is she a letter?"

Renzo smirked. "Even at the best of times it's difficult to make much money as a dancer, and this way she supports the family business. And Nicola is dedicated to Sardinian independence. He is particularly incensed about the new government-built towns on the island," he said turning toward Gina as she returned, presumably with her husband in tow.

"And here is the world-famous Nicola Scarpa," said Renzo, making the obligatory introductions.

Nicola Scarpa towered over Renzo, though they both shared the same slim build. Unlike Renzo's unruly mop of magnificent hair, Nicola's hair was slicked back in a style she had seen on many men around town. His heavy eyebrows almost met in the middle, giving him a perpetually serious countenance. He wore the same uniform as everyone else, though he wore an expensive pair of shoes on his feet, of course.

He surprised them both as he removed two paper bags he had concealed behind his back. With a little bow, he presented one to Ruby and one to Fina. "Early Christmas," he said with a winning smile.

Fina peered into her bag and saw a pair of beautiful aubergine T-strap heels. Fina and Ruby squealed in unison with delight. Ruby held aloft her pair of elegant cream heels for all to admire. Nicola's eye's flickered with pleasure.

"I'm so pleased you find them amenable," he said to Ruby and Fina. "I asked your hotel clerk to help me with the measurements," he added with a mischievous smile. "If you find they are too large or too tight, we will adjust them for you."

Gina Scarpa flitted toward them with a dancer's gait. "I see

Nicola has showered you with gifts," she said with a smile which was a little too broad. It reminded Fina of her primary school teacher, Mrs. Potts, before she had prepared to punish one of her classmates.

After Renzo introduced the two of them again, Gina said, "I expect I'll see you, since Terranova Pausania is a small city."

Renzo shook his lion's mane. "No, Gina, you'll see them sooner than that. They're joining us this weekend on the island."

Gina's newspaper slid through her fingers and fluttered to the floor.

4

Fina scanned the room one more time, imprinting it in her photographic memory. She would miss the lovely Hotel Sardu, and was hesitant to leave. But why? How many people were fortunate enough to be invited to a private island weekend party? She shook her head in dismay – was she becoming spoiled by all these journeys to faraway places with Ruby?

A scratching noise came from the entrance to their room.

Fina crept toward the door as if it might spring open. She squinted through the peephole. Ruby stood outside, holding a suitcase in each hand.

As she opened the door, Ruby dashed to the nearest chair and unloaded her belongings.

"Whew. It's absolutely scorching in the corridor," she said, wiping her face with her favourite blue handkerchief. She turned around and surveyed Fina's suitcase. It was open. What had been packed was neatly folded, but it was half empty. Ruby glanced at her watch. "Let me help you pack, Feens. We need to scarper before James arrives."

Fina nodded and said, "Would you help me collect my bits

and bobs strewn about everywhere? I'm afraid I'll miss something."

Ruby went to work, moving clockwise around the room. Fina held up her new bathing dress in triumph. "I'm thrilled Renzo has a pool! Did you remember to bring yours?"

"Yes, although I'm not sure it will be warm enough for swimming this weekend," she said, then adding, "But you never know. Perhaps we can go for an invigorating dip after a night of wanton behaviour!"

Fina giggled.

Not looking up from her task, Ruby continued, "Did you find Gina's behaviour a little peculiar?"

"Yes!" exclaimed Fina with a fervour which surprised her. "That smile – it reminded me of a leering shark."

Cling, cling.

Fina picked up the receiver on the ancient phone.

"*Prego*," she said.

The voice of the front desk clerk said, "Miss Aubrey-Havelock. A gentleman is here to meet you. His name is James Matua. Shall I ask him to wait?"

"Ah, just a moment," she said glancing at Ruby. She knew Ruby could overhear the conversation.

Ruby mouthed, "Tell him to wait in the lobby."

Fina gave the clerk instructions and began to scuttle around the room, picking up a few last items which she hurled into her luggage. As she sat on her suitcase to force it closed, she said to Ruby, "Why have him wait inside? Shouldn't he wait outside so we can give him the slip?"

"I've already had a look at the stairway in the rear of the hotel. And I've already returned the keys to the desk clerk. The staircase empties out onto an alleyway. Let's hurry before James finds out!"

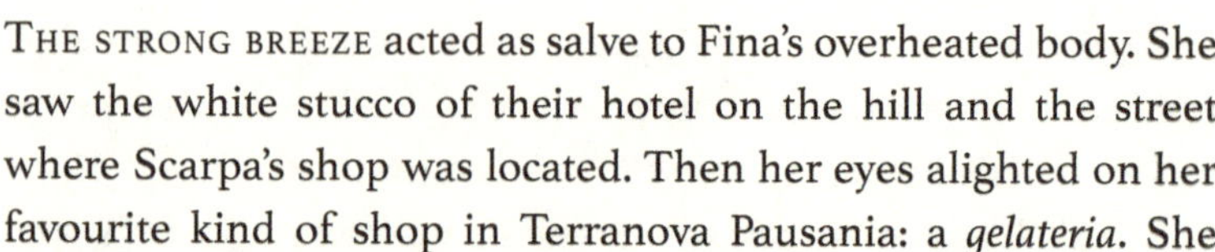

THE STRONG BREEZE acted as salve to Fina's overheated body. She saw the white stucco of their hotel on the hill and the street where Scarpa's shop was located. Then her eyes alighted on her favourite kind of shop in Terranova Pausania: a *gelateria*. She hoped Renzo would offer them homemade gelato this weekend.

She peered over the railing at the people loading their bags of wares, luggage, and crates onto the ferry. One straggler dashed down the street, holding his hand up for the ferry to wait as if it were a London bus. The straggler leapt across the gap between the dock and the boat. A ferry worker shook a finger at him, but then smiled and clapped him on the back. All was forgiven.

The ferry's horn blared, and they were off. Turning away from the churning water, Fina leant against the railing and enjoyed the sun on her face.

"You look like a cat after a nice meal," said Ruby. "Breakfast *was* satisfying. But don't get too comfortable. It's only a few minutes to the point where the ferry stops for Agrodolce."

"I am rather satisfied. Especially since we gave James the slip," she said, pushing her sunglasses back up her nose. She couldn't get used to the blasted things. "Is there an island ferry dock on Agrodolce?"

Ruby shook her head. "Renzo said the island is too small to have a proper ferry dock, so it stops about ten minutes out from Terranova Pausania. Then they take rowing boats from the island to pick us up from the ferry."

"It's already been five minutes. Ought we make our way downstairs?"

They descended to the lower deck of the ferry. Next to the spot heaped with their luggage stood Zenash, Idris and Miss Papas. Idris and Zenash relished their cigarettes as they chattered away. Miss Papas stood in the circle of conversation but stared distractedly out to sea.

Errr ... eeee ... squealed the ferry as they came to an abrupt halt. Fina saved herself from falling backwards as she gripped the railing of the deck. Soon, two bobbing white rowing boats lurched toward the ferry. They resembled pirates preparing to board a ship full of gold doubloons.

Two men disembarked onto the ferry. The first was stocky and muscular. The other was tall and lithe. With a nod toward their group, they began to load each boat with the luggage piled on the deck. Task completed, they motioned to them to follow them into the two boats. Fortunately, they had pulled up to the lowest part of the ferry, so the rope ladder they had to use to climb down to the boats was mercifully short. The other three passengers made their way into the lithe man's boat with little difficulty.

Despite the short distance, Fina was the last to attempt the awkward crawl down the ladder into the stocky man's boat. She stopped midway as a wave hit the ferry.

"You can do it, Feens," said Ruby from behind her. "More waves are coming, so just do your best to lower yourself a few more rungs."

In her nervousness to not make a misstep, she caught her left ankle in the rope. She felt a strong hand hold her back while another disentangled her leg.

The weight of the hand on her back reassured her as her wobbly foot slid into the boat.

"*Grazie mille,*" she said to the stocky man as he helped her sit on a bench near the back of the boat.

They began to row furiously as the ferry blew its horn. Eddies of white water from the departing ferry swirled around them. The wake soon subsided, and their host let his pace of rowing slacken a bit. He stuck out a hand to Fina and declared, "Fabrizio De Sio. Cook."

Fina couldn't tell if Fabrizio was naturally taciturn or if he was uncomfortable speaking English. She suspected it was a bit of both. She offered her hand to him, introducing herself and then Ruby.

Pleasantries over, he began to row again. He plied the oars in slow, rhythmic strokes. He still overtook his furiously rowing competition in the next boat.

Breathing in the clean sea air, Fina surveyed their destination. Agrodolce. The island wasn't far at all from the mainland, but it was far enough that it would be dangerous to undertake the journey in a small rowing boat from shore. The island itself looked like it had different climates. One side was sparse and laid over with brown grass, while the other was lush and green with twisty cork trees – she had learned what they were yesterday. On the end nearest to them, she surveyed a sprawling white villa with a red gabled roof.

She glanced over at the passengers in the other boat. Surprisingly, they all sat as stiff as willow rods, backs barely skimming the sides of the boat. They were transfixed by the approaching island. They reminded her of frozen mice before a cat who is about to pounce. Curious. The sun was shining, the day was beautiful, and they were travelling to a lovely weekend party on a private island. Maybe they were managing their seasickness ... that must be the reason they looked that way.

Unsurprisingly, their boat was the first to dock. Fabrizio leapt out with great agility and tied the front to the wooden post nearest Fina. Ruby and Fina handed their light suitcases to Fabrizio, who gave them the first smile they had seen yet.

5

"*Dilette*! Darlings!" declared a woman in white gauzy chiffon. The layers of her frock – or was it a trouser suit? – were draped artfully around her petite body. She floated toward Ruby and Fina as they made their last steps up the steep hill from the dock.

The woman resembled an imp or a wood sprite, ears peeping out through long, dark hair. And Fina loved imps and wood sprites. She had often been compared to a sprite herself, though she supposed sprites did not have her curves.

Ruby was first in the greeting line. The chiffon-imp woman gripped both of Ruby's shoulders and gave her two firm kisses on each cheek, even though she had to stand on her tiptoes to accomplish this feat.

"You must be Miss Aubrey-Havelock and Miss Dove," she said, beginning to look like she was going to guess who was who. Fina intervened to save them all from the usual mix-up and said, "I'm Fina Aubrey-Havelock. So good to meet you ..."

"Adriana Orso. Adriana is fine. Renzo is my brother. Welcome to our little bit of paradise," she said, sweeping her arm around at the spectacular view of the water and the shores of Sardinia in the distance. As if in answer to Adriana's proclamation, a nearby bird began to sing and the sun peeped out from behind a small puffy cloud. The white villa gleamed as if it had just been scrubbed, partially hidden by the immaculately trimmed hedge lining the perimeter of the house.

Fina had not noticed the person approaching them from behind Adriana. She had materialised from thin air, though her demeanour could not have been more different than Adriana's. Dressed in a shapeless beige linen dress, she stooped a bit as she walked. Adriana spun round and introduced her.

"This is Irene Finlay. She's British, so you all ought to get along nicely," she said as if she were a matchmaker. Irene held out a hand to Fina. Fina clasped the cold hand which gradually squeezed her like a boa who hadn't been fed for a week. Fina did her best to turn her wince into a smile. "Pleased to meet you, Miss Finlay."

Introductions complete, they began their ascent to the villa entrance. Fabrizio had disappeared with their luggage. Adriana twirled her way into the cool and dark entrance hall. "Welcome to our home. Please treat it as your own during your stay here. We are informal people who cannot believe we are fortunate enough to live in such a palace. Every day we are here, I say to Renzo, 'when will the real owners return home?'" she said with a grin.

Still twirling steadily like a ballet dancer in a musical jewellery box, she continued. "Because we have no idea how to run a proper household, we have Ruggero. I suppose he'd be called a butler. Or ... what is the name of the man who works for another man?"

"Valet," supplied Ruby.

"Ah yes, a valet. Such a funny name for a person, don't you think? Yes, so Ruggero helps out with all sorts of things around the house. You met the cook, Fabrizio. He is an artist, so we allow him his artistic temperament. You see, I understand these things as I am an artist myself."

"What kind of artist?" asked Fina.

"A serious painter," intoned Irene from behind Fina. Blast the woman. Why was she sneaking up on them? Fina glanced behind her and saw bare feet with blue toenails peeking out from the long beige dress. No wonder she was so quiet.

Adriana smiled at Irene. "Irene is a good friend and an art critic. She works at the Tate Gallery in London."

"Are you a curator there?" asked Ruby.

Irene shook her large head. "I do occasionally assist in designing shows, but mostly I spot forgeries."

"Forgeries?" spluttered Fina. "But how thrilling!"

"I'm afraid it's a mundane task most days. It takes enormous concentration. But occasionally I do get an exciting case. Just the other day—"

"Darlings, let's get you settled," interrupted Adriana. "Fabrizio will have put your luggage in your rooms."

Ruby and Fina gave her obliging smiles and followed Adriana up the marble steps to the first floor. She watched Ruby nearly hit her head on one of the low beams. Must be an old house. Cool and warm breezes floated across the hallway at cross purposes with one another. This part of the villa smelt like an old library – a comforting sensation.

They reached a door with a small oil painting of what appeared to be a fat game hen. "It's a *piccola otarda*," said Adriana, reading Fina's mind. "Quite tasty," she said, removing a large ring of keys from somewhere underneath the folds of her white chiffon. "This is Ruby's room." She opened the door and waved to Fina for her to follow. On the next door hung an oil painting of an olive tree. Adriana wiggled the key in the lock for a minute before it gave way.

The room was small but well proportioned. Everything had

a niche – the wardrobe, dressing table and even the jug of water in the corner. And it felt lived in, so Fina didn't have that feeling she was inhaling a stranger's room – like she did so often on these weekend parties.

"I'll leave you in peace," said Adriana. "Please toddle around the grounds if that's appealing to you. We don't have a set schedule. We'll have *aperitivi*, – what you call starters – at some point, but it all depends on when everyone arrives."

Fina grinned and nodded as Adriana floated out of the room. This was one of her favourite moments of travelling. Unpacking and anticipating everything that was to come this weekend. Just as she lifted her suitcase onto the bed, a tap came from the door.

It was Ruby, of course. "I've already finished unpacking. That's the benefit of travelling to warm climates." She went to the window and opened it, breathing in deeply. "We have a lovely view of the sea and the mainland in the distance," she said as Fina joined her at the window.

"It's absolutely spiffing. Notice that large boat?" Fina said, pointing her finger at a white object bobbing in the water near the shore of the mainland.

"It must be Renzo's boat," said Ruby. "He said he'd take his own boat over with the remaining guests. I'll help you unpack so we can explore a bit before he arrives. It will be difficult to sneak out of the villa once everyone is here."

"What's that?" asked Ruby, pointing to a small suitcase near the bed.

Fina peered over the white counterpane. "I'm not sure. It's not mine. Perhaps Fabrizio accidentally loaded someone else's luggage into our boat," she said as she bent over to unsnap the case. Opening it revealed a jumble of toiletries, yellow and red scarves, pens and notebooks. Fina drew out a tomato-red frilly dress. Then a daringly cut mauve number which shimmered in the light.

Ruby scooped up a green notebook from the suitcase and opened it.

"Ruby!" said Fina. "That's someone's personal notebook. You ought not to read it."

"People like us need all the information we can gather on our guests. It's good practice," she said, flipping through the pages lined with small, neat handwriting. "Besides, I stop reading if it's too intimate."

Fina stood with her hands on her hips. "Well? What have you discovered?"

Ruby held up her forefinger in the air. "It's Nefeli Papas' suitcase."

"That's the woman who was with Zenash and Idris."

"Her small, neat handwriting is such a contrast to the disarray of her suitcase," said Ruby, nodding affirmation. "She's writing in her notebook about attending an accounting meeting," she sighed, turning to the next page. A piece of paper fluttered to the floor.

Fina picked it up and began to read aloud, translating from Italian as best she could:

Carlotta,

I know everything now. You will pay.

v.

"See? We shouldn't be reading other people's letters," said Fina as she angrily stuffed the letter back into the notebook.

Ruby tapped her teeth, ignoring Fina's outrage. "I wonder who 'v' could be. Ominous. Why does Nefeli have a letter to a person named Carlotta in her case?"

Fina gave out a little grunt of frustration. "I don't know who 'v' is and I don't care. Neither should you."

"But Feens, this is all good practice." She moved on to

another subject. "It's difficult to believe this is Nefeli's suitcase, especially because the note is addressed to Carlotta." She paused. "Of course, I remember now, Carlotta Visconti is a guest this weekend. A famous opera singer."

"Then that makes it even more puzzling," said Fina, touching a pink ruffle sticking out of the suitcase. "Why does she have these frilly dresses in here? They're lovely, but not her style. Nefeli was wearing trousers and a blouse when we saw her earlier today."

"People are never what they seem, are they?"

Ruby repacked the suitcase and placed it outside the door. Fina set to work unfurling her three summer frocks, which she sprayed with water from the water jug to remove the wrinkles. Within two minutes the rest of the contents of the suitcase had been emptied.

Glancing out of the window, Fina noticed the boat had moved much closer to the island. Was it moving that fast? It must be an optical illusion from the water. She was gripped by a sudden urge to dash out of the villa before it reached the shore.

6

———————

For the second time that day, Ruby and Fina tiptoed down the backstairs to exit a building unnoticed. Fina wriggled her toes with the pleasure which comes from wearing open-toed sandals in a warm climate. Warm as toast. She put on her sunglasses once more and nodded at Ruby that they should begin their adventure.

The creaky backstairs let out onto a small terrace surrounded by shrubs. A table and chairs sat to one side – a perfect place to mull over the day's events. But what would they need to mull over? After all, Ruby had been asked here to meet with Renzo, not solve a case. She was surprised by the twinge of regret she felt at not having a case to solve with Ruby.

"There's a small pathway on this side of the terrace, Feens. Let's see where it leads," said Ruby. Sure enough, a small, well-worn pathway wound around the cliff near the rear of the villa. They set off, single file. Soon the path widened enough for them to walk side by side.

"Now that we've arrived, will you tell me more about why Renzo asked you here?" asked Fina. "You know how your secretiveness drives me barmy," she said in a playful voice.

"You're right, Feens. I know it can be insufferable, but it's how I am. Sometimes I feel that if I tell you these things, it's as if they become more real, more concrete. Sometimes I don't want them to become real yet because I begin to run through all the scenarios – where everything goes pear-shaped."

"Really? You always seem so calm and collected on the outside."

"It's because I control what I allow to bother me and what I try to shut out of my mind," she said, adjusting her sunglasses. "Besides, my calm exterior is often just that – a calm exterior. As for the reason why we're here, you read the letter Renzo sent me. That's all I know. It's clear he wants to discuss our activities, but I'm not sure from what angle. He is deeply involved in the Italian left, but I suspect his invitation was prompted by the Italian invasion of Ethiopia."

"Hmmm ... perhaps. Do you think the other guests are involved in some way?"

"I don't know. The Scarpas are the only ones who have a tie to the fashion business, apart from Carlotta – the opera singer I mentioned. She's married to a leather magnate. It must be the reason Renzo knows her."

"I suppose Irene is here as Adriana's friend, and Idris and Zenash are here because they're artistically inclined," said Fina, swatting a fly away from her face.

"Yes. That leaves Miss Papas. Why would Renzo invite an accountant? She seems out of step with this crowd. But that might be because we haven't met everyone else yet."

"What a splendid view!" cried Fina as she pointed to the vast sea which opened up as they turned a corner. To their right, Fina surveyed the small bobbing boats of Terranova Pausania harbour. To her left, the calm, shimmering sea stretched out for miles. When she glanced downwards, she spied the dock and myriad pathways crisscrossing the landscape like the roots of an oak tree.

"It's spectacular, isn't it? This is our best adventure yet, Feens," Ruby said.

Fina nodded. "It is. And I'm glad we have all this water between James and us. Ha! I'd like to watch him try to track us from the shore with a pair of binoculars!" she laughed.

Ruby chuckled. "Yes, he must be exasperated with us. We're always on the move." She glanced over the cliff and began to sway.

Fina grabbed her arm. "Are you ill? Why were you swaying?"

"Thanks. I forgot that sometimes I have a touch of vertigo from heights. Glad you were here to steady me," she said, holding her head.

"Who's down there?" asked Fina, pointing to a figure in a large, floppy hat. She stopped herself. "Don't look. I'll tell you when they come a little closer," she paused. "Now you can look."

Ruby squinted. "By her gait, I'd say it's Irene."

Fina felt an unjustified and unbidden urge to turn around and run back to the villa. What was wrong with her?

"Let's catch her up," said Ruby. Dutifully, she traipsed after Ruby toward an inevitable collision with Irene.

Irene removed her enormous hat and squinted at the two of them. "Lovely here, isn't it? I try to walk around the island at least once a day while I'm here. Good for the art critic's soul. It often goes sour inside the walls of the museum." She turned back toward the villa and then spun around as if an idea had just occurred to her. "Let me show you a secret spot."

7

———

Without waiting for their approval, Irene took off at a fast clip and took a sharp right down a hill. Ruby and Fina made little hops in between a fast trot to keep up with Irene. Soon, a small shack emerged from the golden brown of the hillside. Irene pointed as if it were an oasis in the desert.

"Isn't it wonderful?" asked Irene.

Fina wasn't sure if she meant the shack or the view. She hoped it was the view because the shack resembled an outpost in the Great War. They both smiled politely and trundled down after Irene to the entrance.

As they entered, it became clear that this was what Irene meant by wonderful. The interior was a study in contrast from the exterior. Every detail had been seen to, from the embroidered counterpane on the small bed in the corner, to the artful blue and red flower arrangement in a cool emerald vase. Near the window stood an easel with a half-finished oil painting. That must be the smell. The strong smell of oil paints. Despite the closed door and window, there was a slight breeze which weakened the odour. The painting was a delightful study of Terranova Pausania harbour. Though the painting appeared dry, the palette of paints looked shiny and wet.

"This is Adriana's studio," said Irene with great pride. "Sometimes she lets me come here to ruminate and write."

"Are you a writer as well? How talented," said Ruby.

Irene stared down at her blue toenails. "No, no. I write for myself sometimes. I find it soothing."

Ruby nodded absently and then stared at a necklace draped over the easel. "What an unusual pendant," said Ruby, stroking the two porcelain hens dangling from a silver chain.

"Oh, that's Adriana's talisman. It's the Sardinian symbol of industry – she says it helps her work rapidly and steadily when she paints. And my, does she paint a great deal. Adriana is careful to be in tune with her surroundings. I wish I could do the same, but I'm afraid I often get lost in my head," she said with a bitter note in her voice.

Odd, thought Fina. She hadn't observed many paintings in the studio. Maybe collectors had already snapped them up – or they were stored elsewhere. She imagined the climate wasn't the best for painting storage.

"I can understand that," said Fina. "I have a hard time quieting the voices in my head."

Gulp. Ruby and Irene glanced at Fina quizzically.

"What I mean is – selkies and kelpies – it did sound a little rum, didn't it? I mean that I often get caught up with worries."

Irene's face relaxed. "Ah, that's precisely what I meant!"

Somehow, the tension rose in the little shack. As if Ruby also sensed it, she said, "I'm afraid I ought to be getting back. I'd like to rest a bit before we all meet up again this evening."

Looking relieved herself, Irene led them out of the studio. As they began to walk back to the villa, Ruby said, "Does Adriana always paint in her studio down there?"

"No, she had a few spots in the villa – inside and outside –

where she paints. She's flexible, but when she paints with oils she often goes to the studio by the sea. You see, Renzo cannot stand the smell of oils. He's sensitive."

As they came to the crest of the little hill, Fina spied a patch of blue in front of them, directly behind the villa. A pool! It was so inviting after this outing.

"Is the pool still swimmable in November?" asked Fina with rising anticipation in her voice as they scampered down the hill.

"Go ahead, dip your hand in," said Irene, swishing her own hand about in the water.

Fina and Ruby did so. "Not bad, I suppose," said Fina. "Better than Brighton."

Irene and Ruby chuckled. "Yes, I often go for a swim in the afternoon after it's warmed up. It's certainly invigorating. If I do that, I find I don't need a nap."

As she stood up from the pool, Fina watched Renzo approaching with a friend in tow. Fina appreciated his change of footwear into brown leather sandals. "Welcome! Welcome to the Villa Sprezzatura!" he said, embracing Ruby and Fina. He merely gave a polite nod toward Irene. Hmmm. Interesting.

Though it was not harder to be taller than Renzo, the man behind him positively loomed over the shoe designer. He, too, wore a fantastic pair of shoes, though the brogues appeared less comfortable than sandals. His most distinctive feature was his glorious hair. It was a masterpiece of cut, style, and pomade. It added a good two to three inches to his height. Unlike Renzo's magnificent mane, this man's hair resembled a perfectly mani-cured hedge from Versailles.

He leant over and clasped Ruby's hand, clicking his heels at the same time. Deuced peculiar. "I understand you are Miss Dove," he said. Then he spun on his heel toward Fina. "And you must be Miss Aubrey-Havelock. Delighted to meet you both," he said with another little bow.

Renzo clapped him on the small of the back, because it was about as far as he could reach. "Let me introduce Silvio Rametti, my private doctor who sees to my various illnesses. He was born in London to Italian parents and studied there, so you three ought to have something to chat about."

Ruby put her hand over her heart. "Are you ill, Renzo? I'm so sorry. Perhaps we ought to return to the mainland."

"No, no, dear Ruby. I just have—"

"He has a long list of ailments which I attend to," said the doctor. "Nothing which cannot be maintained with a little attention."

Ruby sighed. "That's a relief, but do let us know if we're a bother this weekend, Renzo."

Renzo's hands flew up in an embracing gesture toward Ruby and Fina. "Rubbish, as you English say. Balderdash!" he said with a wink, clearly enjoying the way the words rolled around on his tongue. "You two are most welcome," he said, before lowering his voice. "And I have much to discuss with you when we find the time. But now, we must enjoy ourselves! Everyone has now arrived. Adriana and I have a special treat for you all."

He peered down at his watch. "I've told everyone to convene here at the pool in an hour. Then you shall see!"

THE COOL WATER of the bath jolted Fina out of her stupor. She peered out the small window at the end of the bath. A little patch of sea peeped through above the olive trees. Fortunately, the cold set in quickly, so she jumped out, dried herself, and slipped into her dressing gown. She padded down the hallway toward her bedroom.

As she passed the room with the small oil painting of a goat, she heard a scraping noise. Pausing to listen, she decided it must be a guest rearranging the furniture in their room. She hadn't moved a stick of furniture in her own room. It was just perfect.

Once she arrived in her bedroom, she vacillated between choosing a more formal silk evening gown or a simple sleeveless navy frock. Many of the guests were glamorous, but she also sensed Renzo preferred informality. In the end, she opted for the navy frock. She could save the gown if there were a more formal occasion.

"Feens! Are you in there?" came Ruby's voice from the corridor.

Fina went to open the door. Ruby had also opted for a simple, but always elegant, gown of silver and black. She eyed Fina with approval. "Glad we're in agreement."

"What did Renzo mean by a special treat?"

"No idea. But there is something devilishly peculiar about this house party."

"Do you mean the doctor? Or Renzo's illness? Or Irene's blue toenails?"

Ruby tapped her teeth. "Well, those are oddities, I agree. But it's something about the party as a whole. I believe we've met almost everyone. Have you noticed anything about where everyone is from, originally?"

"Let's see. Irene and Silvio are originally from London. Miss Papas is from Rhodes, Idris is from Tripoli, Zenash is from Addis Ababa, and the Scarpas are Sardinian. And I don't know about the valet and cook. Nor Renzo and Adriana, though I assume they're from Italy or Sardinia."

"Precisely. Rhodes, Libya, Ethiopia and Sardinia. What do those places have in common with one another, my friend the political historian?"

Fina's eyes widened. "They've all been colonised by Italy."

8

———

Whoosh.

A torrent of water flooded underneath Fina's door into the room. She and Ruby stood transfixed. Shaking her head, Ruby leapt over the small stream and swung open the door.

Ruggero, the valet, resembled a rabbit caught in the act of stealing carrots. He held a rusty metal bucket in one hand. Fina supposed it was empty since its contents must have spread on the floor. He dropped the bucket with a loud clang and cried, "I am so sorry, ladies! Please do forgive me. I was bringing this down to Fabrizio when I slipped and nearly tumbled. The water spilt out. I will clean it!" he exclaimed as he ran down the corridor toward the stairs.

"Odd," said Ruby to Fina. "Why would he be retrieving water for the first floor? They have indoor plumbing."

Fina shook her head. "He must have been listening at our door, and slipped. I'd say we ought to stay, but what's the point? He'll try to make more excuses when he returns. The damage isn't too extensive," she said, leaving the door open a crack as she also hopped over the puddle. "Let's ignore it and find out what this surprise might be downstairs."

"Wait a moment, Feens," said Ruby, moving into a squatting position on the floor. She scooped something up.

She held her dripping quarry aloft as if it were a soiled undergarment. A small leather-bound notebook.

"Must have slipped out of Ruggero's pocket during the kerfuffle," said Fina, taking it from Ruby so she could adjust her dress.

She shook the notebook, spraying Ruby with water.

"Thanks, Feens," said Ruby. Then she giggled. "Let's take a look."

"Really? Ought we?"

Ruby gave an ever-so-slight roll of her eyes. Then her eyes softened. "I'm glad I have you as my moral compass. But remember, he was listening at our door."

"I suppose so. What does it say?"

Ruby flipped through the pages. "It's empty except for the first entry," she said, holding it so the two of them could read it together. "Can you translate? Your Italian is better than mine."

Fina began to read aloud slowly:

XIII

R & A invited artists to villa. CV also invited. Weather for weekend expected to be partly sunny, partly stormy. F acting peculiarly.

"Maybe he's making notes to himself so he remembers what he needs to do?"

Ruby nodded steadily. "It's plausible."

Fina began to move toward the staircase. "Let's go downstairs and return it to him."

"Not for the moment," said Ruby, quickly popping into her bedroom.

"Why ever not?"

"If we return it, he'll sense we read it. Then he'll be suspicious of us – he already is, clearly, if he's listening at our door. If we don't give it to him, then he'll think he misplaced it," she said, waving her hands. When Ruby waved her hands, it was a sure sign she was uncomfortable with whatever she was saying. "Besides, there was only one entry in the notebook. We'll leave it for him when we leave the island."

"Right you are, Ruby Dove," said Fina.

They snaked their way down the curved staircase into the entrance hall. The sounds of a Victrola playing Carlos Gardel tinkled in the background. Fina shook her head thinking about his tragic death a few months ago in a plane crash. She loved the drama of tango.

The entrance hall was empty, so they followed the music to the terrace. Fina saw a flash of tangerine orange overlaid with blackout of the corner of her eye. A woman in a foamy orange, shoulder-baring gown danced with Renzo, who was now dressed in a long black linen shirt and matching black trousers. He wore black canvas boating shoes. The woman towered above him due to her natural height, along with artificial help from a pair of daring heels. Fina's mouth hung open as she stared at those shoes. In between swishes of her dress around Renzo, she noted the heel of the black shoe must have been over two inches in height and razor-thin. Fina's heart pounded with every turn, as she was sure the woman would topple over into a great heap of orange sherbet onto the terrace or into the nearby pool.

Their tango complete, the woman in orange bowed while she propped her arm on Renzo, who also followed suit. Fina felt the mismatch in height, along with the stupendous heels, made this all rather marvellous. Apparently, she was not the only one to think so, as thunderous applause and yelps of approval echoed around the terrace.

Ruby dashed up to the couple as soon as they came to a complete halt. Fina realised by Ruby's stare that she, too, was fascinated by the heels. Fina followed. Renzo winked at the two of them. "I expect I know what you two were staring at, and it wasn't the fabulous turns on the floor," he said, motioning to the woman's feet.

"First, let me introduce to you Carlotta Visconti: opera singer and tango dancer," he said, also introducing Ruby and Fina.

"So pleased to meet you, Miss Visconti," said Ruby breath-lessly. "A stupendous performance. But I must say I'm even more taken with your shoes!" She paused, possibly realising it sounded dismissive. "What I mean is that Fina and I are fashion aficiona-dos, and we're here to learn as much as we can from Renzo about shoe design. That's why I'm so smitten with your heels."

Carlotta bestowed them with a beautiful, if alarmingly toothy, smile. She leant over Ruby as if she might be deciding whether she'd be a tasty morsel for dinner. "No trouble at all, Miss Dove. And it's actually Mrs Visconti, though I'd much prefer Carlotta."

Ruby scanned the terrace, presumably searching for Mr Visconti.

Renzo intervened. "Mr Visconti is in Rome, where the Viscontis live. He's a leather magnate. Perhaps you're familiar with his name?"

Fina's photographic memory unleashed itself. She remem-bered a headline about politics and an Italian leather business-man. Visconti ... Vito. That was it. "Vito Visconti, of course!" she exclaimed, as if she had just won the Irish Sweeps.

Carlotta now scrutinised Fina. Before, she had merely waved a hand at her. "Why yes, Miss Aubrey-Havelock, that's my husband," she sighed, and stared at her perfectly manicured red-lacquered nails. "He's forever off on business trips, so I come often to visit Renzo here in his delightful villa." She lifted her long foamy skirt off the wooden deck to reveal her heels. "And he always has a pair of shoes for me."

Renzo sat down on his haunches and gestured toward the shoes. "Though the real treat comes later, I couldn't wait to show you these," he said, looking up at Ruby. "I'm still settling on the name for them. They're so thin, I'm calling them *sotille*, but I'm not entirely satisfied with the name yet."

Ruby leant over to look. Fina surveyed the rest of the guests on the terrace glancing over at them as they huddled around Carlotta's dress.

Renzo and Ruby returned to their standing posture. Ruby said, "They're rather like daggers, aren't they? In Italian it's *stiletto*, correct?"

Fina smiled, remembering how the two of them had frantically crammed in as much studying of Italian as possible in the weeks before their trip. Fina had studied Italian before, which meant she was ahead of Ruby. Fortunately for them, everyone spoke enough English on the island – with the exception of Fabrizio – that they didn't need to worry.

Renzo's eyes lit up. "Ruby, my darling! But it's a perfect name for them. Stilettos!"

Carlotta nodded her approval. "They are rather dangerous, aren't they, Renzo?"

"But of course! They are not only dangerous to wear – because you're likely to tipple and topple in them – but they also look dangerous," he said, rubbing his hands together. "You've already made your visit worthwhile," he said to Ruby and Fina. "And here I thought I'd teach you something."

"Are they ready to be modelled soon?" Ruby asked. Fina

could tell she was slightly embarrassed by the attention. She had backed away almost imperceptibly from Renzo.

"Alas, no. I'm afraid the time is not right. Certainly not in Italy right now. Conservatism – I don't mean the political kind – is sweeping Europe right now. I'll be saving these for when the time is right. You see, that is half the battle in designing shoes or clothes. Timing is of the essence," he said, with his fingers pinched together as if he were describing the delicate bouquet of wine.

Adriana swept up behind them and tapped Renzo's shoulder. "Renzi, I know you could talk about shoes all night. But the guest's stomachs are beginning to, how do you say? Rumble. That's it – rumble and grumble."

Renzo nodded, though he still stared at Carlotta's shoes peeping out from beneath her dress. "Where's Ruggero?" he asked.

Thump. Thump.

Fina spun round and watched Ruggero thumping in behind her. He had a knack for hearing his name but sounded like an elephant casually wandering onto the terrace. She wondered why he made such a racket. He was tall and thin, so it couldn't be his bulk.

"Yes, Renzo. Dinner is ready on the terrace overlooking the sea."

9

———

Wine glasses in hand, guests traipsed along a pebbled path around the villa's perimeter to another terrace. Fina reflected on how divine it would be to be able to eat outside all the time. Not a possibility in London much of the year.

Meoowww. Skiiiish.

Fina stumbled over something furry. Her wine glass went flying over the small cliff to the right of the pathway. She heard it smash into a million shards.

Irene, who was behind her, grabbed Fina's arm so she didn't go flying over the cliff to meet the same fate as her wine glass.

"Wretched animals," she said. "That was Diva. I'm sure Divo is not far behind, so be careful in case he decides to cross your path as well. They're siblings."

Fina spotted a tuxedo cat slinking in front of her, clearly on the hunt. "What does Divo look like? I must admit I'm keen on kitties, even when they unintentionally try to kill me."

Irene shook her head. "Give me a dog any day over these narcissistic beasts. You can tell Divo and Diva apart from their markings. Divo is solid black, while Diva is a tuxedo."

Fina bent down and petted Divo, who had also sneaked up

behind her. He gave her an obliging purr and then scurried off after Diva.

The long table on the terrace was already set. Cold dishes of olives and meats already lined the centre of the arrangement. Fina watched Diva loping toward the food, glancing side to side as if the action would protect her from being seen. Adriana shooed away the cat before she could abscond with the prosciutto.

Fina sat between Idris and Nefeli. The woman had an appetite. Good lord she could tuck it away, thought Fina, as she watched her munch on bread and olives between sips of wine. Her sunken frame indicated she hadn't eaten much in weeks, if not months. Perhaps she hadn't. Mustn't judge, she chided herself for the thousandth time. Besides it being morally objectionable, it didn't help her develop sleuthing and spying skills.

Idris topped up Fina's glass with the local Nepente wine. "This is delicious," he said as he sipped his own glass. "How do you find Sardinia? Is this your first time visiting?"

Fina's only response was a nod as her mouth was full of olives. Swallowing, she replied, "Yes. This is my first time in Sardinia and Italy. It's lovely. And you?"

He spat out a pit into a nearby bowl. "No, I've been to Italy many times, though I've never been to Sardinia. Sicily is only 500 kilometres from Tripoli, though I haven't lived in Tripoli for a while. London is my home, at least temporarily."

"Why temporarily?" As usual, a question just popped into her head and she had to ask it. "Because of the political situation?"

He stroked his chin. "How astute of you. Do you follow politics?"

"Yes, I read history at Oxford, but I'm most interested in political history."

Idris' eyes widened. "Really, that's most edifying. It would be easy to pretend the world is not falling down about our ears," he said, twisting the stem of his wine glass. "How can I blame anyone for thinking it? So much of it is beyond our control."

"Did you leave when Italy declared the country to be 'Italian Libya' last year?"

This time, he spat the pit into the bowl with a great deal of force. "Yes. The Blackshirts arrived. They had already colonised Libya in 1901, but Mussolini ushered in an entirely different era. I had to leave."

"Were you forced out?"

"In a manner of speaking, yes. I'm Berber, but more importantly in this case, I'm Jewish," he said in a whisper. "Fortunately, I was known enough in London that I was able to slip out of the country unnoticed. My architect and design skills made sure I had enough to eat," he said, voice rising as Adriana caught his eye.

"Yes, let's eat!" exclaimed Adriana, sitting at the end of the table next to Idris. She rose from her seat and began to serve the main course with Renzo and Ruggero's assistance. Fina couldn't believe they were going to eat even more after the plentiful cold dishes.

Ruggero slid a plate with an enormous thin, crispy sheet of bread in front of her. Fina grinned. She loved the *carasau* bread served at almost every meal.

"This is *malloreddus*," said Adriana as she placed a dish of shell-shaped pasta on the table, dolloped with a healthy portion of grated cheese.

Renzo placed a dish with red sauce next to her. Fina smelt the sea. Must be fish or shellfish.

With gusto, Fina dug into her plate piled high with shell pasta. The wine had made her hungry. Near silence enveloped the table – as though they were monks gathered for dinner. Indeed, a shared meal on a night like this felt sacred. Waves lapped against the rock, interspersed with the persistent yet lazy chirp of cicadas.

Renzo, arms lowered on the table, smiled at his sister across from him. He definitely appeared to be enjoying himself. And yet. Fina noticed for the first time his eyelid twitched. Maybe it was just a condition. Next to him sat Silvio, who blocked the view of Renzo with his hair every time he leant over his plate. He began to converse with Renzo. All Fina could hear were the words "aches" and "mood." Must be something about the latest treatments for one of his ailments. As she chewed absently on the last forkful from her plate, she wondered what these ailments could be. He looked the picture of health.

"Is this your first time travelling to the Mediterranean?" asked Nefeli, settling her hands in her lap for a temporary rest from her food. She peered at Fina with genuine curiosity.

"Why yes. Though I've never considered travelling to the Mediterranean as a sea – I usually think about travelling to individual countries. But you're quite right, the Mediterranean itself ties together so many places."

Nefeli nodded vigorous approval. "Precisely. We have representatives here not only from Sardinia, Italy and Rhodes like myself, but from Tripoli, like Idris. We share strong connections." Nodding toward Zenash, she said, "As you are a student at the world-famous Oxford, you must also know of the ancient relationships between Ethiopia and Greece."

Zenash must have heard the word "Ethiopia" because her head perked up from her plate immediately. "Nefeli is correct. It's a story Europeans often like to ignore. The idea that places in Africa, like Ethiopia, are the cradles of civilisation."

Nefeli and Zenash began to spar in a spirited debate about whether the Horn of Africa or Greece was the cradle of so-called civilisation.

Across the table, Ruby and Gina were engaged in a lively

conversation about ballet shoes. Gina was nodding and smiling, but Fina couldn't help but notice it looked like a smirk.

Nicola's hair had lost its stick from the pomade and was now flying around rapidly as he made an emphatic point about football to Ruggero. Adriana and Irene were whispering but occasionally pointed across the table at Carlotta. She sat remarkably still next to Renzo. She would shovel a forkful of food into her mouth and then set it down with a sigh.

Fabrizio came into view, carrying a large earthenware tray with a top. He set it down on a side table and pulled up a chair in between Irene and Adriana. Their voices became louder as they sang their praises of Fabrizio's culinary skills.

"Fabrizio's lamb and artichokes are the talk of Sardinia!" said Irene, raising a glass. Fabrizio blushed.

Fina translated his reply as "Not the best time of year for it, but still delicious."

She nodded and smiled at Fabrizio as she took a first bite of lamb. He nodded his approval.

Ouch.

Selkies and kelpies. Ruby had kicked her in the shin. She glanced over at Ruby, who gracefully moved her fork on the table toward Idris. What in heaven's name was she supposed to talk to him about? Oh well, she'd give it a go.

"What are you planning to do this weekend? Are there things to see on the island?"

"I haven't been here before, but I've heard there are some archaeological sites. Other than that, I plan to stroll or go for a swim in the morning, draw a bit, and then take a nap in the afternoon."

"You mean sketch for your work?"

"A London millionaire asked me to design a special house for his dogs."

Clink. Fina's fork dropped onto the plate in surprise.

"You mean a doghouse?"

Idris smiled. "An actual house, not a small doghouse. I initially dismissed the idea, but I had no other work at the time. What money I do have I send to my family in Tripoli." Idris snatched a piece of prosciutto with a fork from a nearby plate and dropped it on the other side of his chair. Fina spied a cat's tail wrap around his chair leg. She heard the faint sound of happy munching.

"How do you know Renzo? Why did he invite you? Do you know anyone else here?"

Idris set down his fork. "You're rather inquisitive, aren't you? I met Renzo through a friend of a friend. Renzo travels to London from time to time, and he invited me to join him at one of these weekend parties. Those of us who live in exile form a relatively small community in London. Everyone is acquainted with everyone else in some way. That's how I first met Zenash," he said, gesturing across the table. She stopped her banter and gave him a smile.

How curious. Her eavesdropping on the hotel terrace this morning clearly indicated that this was the first time Zenash and Idris had met.

Bang.

Carlotta thumped down a bottle of wine near her plate. Fina couldn't tell if this was the effect of too much wine or if it was an intentional gesture of outrage. It was difficult to gauge from the impassive look on her face. But when her eyes slid toward Renzo, she realised it was a message.

Renzo pulled back his chair and stood. Despite his petite stature, he had a commanding presence. "Let us move to the pool area. Carlotta has agreed to sing for us. We also have delicious fruit to complete the meal."

10

Juice from an orange dribbled down Fina's chin. She wiped her face with a napkin before it escaped onto her frock. Without looking up from her book, Ruby picked up her own napkin and handed it to Fina. She was so accustomed to Fina's susceptibility to accidents that her behaviour toward it had become automatic.

Candles dotted the perimeter of the pool. Carlotta moved into position. Fina peered up at the stars. A perfectly clear and magical evening, even as she shivered. She leant over to Ruby and said, "I need my shawl. Shall I fetch yours?"

Ruby smiled and shook her head.

Although the concert had not yet begun, Fina tiptoed through the fluttering curtains into the dim light of the drawing room. And then her snooping instinct arose. Everyone, including Fabrizio and Ruggero – even the cats – was lounging on the terrace. It wouldn't hurt to have a little look around. After all, she had to improve her sleuthing skills on behalf of their political activities.

Without a clue where she was going, she let intuition be her guide around the ground floor. She drifted past the front door, behind the staircase and toward a room with an ornately carved door. Perhaps it was the library. Or study?

Light pressure was all that was needed to let the door creak open. Fortunately, Carlotta's superb rendition of a Puccini aria covered the noise.

An open window at the far end of the room filtered in enough light to let her find her bearings. This must be Renzo's or Adriana's study. Oil paintings of bucolic scenes lined the walls. Sketches of shoes on a side table confirmed the study must belong to Renzo. The desk was neither neat nor disorderly. A stiletto shoe stood at one end. Fina was careful not to bump it or shake the desk, for it would surely topple over. Touching nothing, she tiptoed around the perimeter, scanning everything with intense focus. Receipts littered one end of the desk, sketches another.

One drawer sat at an angle, halfway open. She bent down, craned her neck and peered inside. It brimmed with tonic bottles, pill boxes and tinctures. The bottle nearest the opening read "nerve and brain elixir." Must be for Renzo's ailments. She pulled on the handle of the drawer on the opposite side of the desk. It was jammed or locked. Either way, she didn't want to risk leaving a trail, so she left the drawer alone.

And then her heart stopped.

As Fina lifted her head, she saw large block letters proclaiming "Ruby Dove" atop a stack of files on his desk.

Had she and Ruby walked into a trap? Wetting one finger, she flipped through the file. It contained a dossier about Ruby's life and political activities. Her heart skipped again when her eyes fixed on the name emblazoned across one memo.

Ian Clavering.

Creak.

In a flash, Fina seized the memo with Ian's name, shut the folder and crouched on the floor behind the desk. She knew it was better to be a coward for a minute than dead for the rest of your life. As she held her breath, a stray cat hair tickled her nose. Must. Not. Sneeze.

From the gentle tapping noise, she decided the intruder must be someone in heels.

Whoever it was, they were rifling through the papers in a methodical, careful way. This person was also moving around the desk in a clockwise motion, as Fina had herself. She was done for.

The heels stopped at the far end of the desk. The person's breath became rapid. A shuffling noise sounded like they were stuffing something in a bag or pocket.

Click. Click.

The heels came closer.

Nefeli peered over the desk.

"*O Theé mou!* You gave me a fright," she said, holding her hand over her chest. "What the devil are you doing crouched behind the desk?"

Fina's first instinct was to make excuses. But Ruby had taught her to go on the offensive in these situations. She stood up as gracefully as she could. "I'll ask the same of you."

Nefeli's eyebrows rose and her mouth curled. She put her splayed hands on the desk and leant over toward Fina. "I've agreed to help Renzo with his accounts. That's the reason I'm here this weekend. I decided to have a head start by poking around a bit. Carlotta's voice is sublime, but it's a little too piercing for me." She paused. "And you?"

A familiar warmth laced its way up Fina's neck. "I'm afraid I'm a terrible snoop. It's a condition. My doctor diagnosed me as compulsive. It's like kleptomania, except I don't steal things."

"I see," she said drily. She tapped her well-manicured fingers on the stack of files.

"You won't tell anyone, will you? It's dreadfully embarrassing."

"Well ..."

"I'll be sure not to tell anyone you were in here, either," Fina paused. "Not that you needed an excuse, of course."

Nefeli crossed her arms and surveyed Fina. "I suppose. But don't expect me to cover up if you are caught again!"

11

———

Like a bull charging ahead, Fina rushed out of the door, head bent down.

Soon her head collided with a body. Idris.

The corner of Idris' mouth lifted in a wry smile. "Where are you off to in such a hurry? Isn't this supposed to be a relaxing weekend?"

Her eyes locked with his. Involuntarily, she told herself. "I felt queasy and dizzy, so I'm afraid I became a little disorientated," she said, clutching her stomach. Selkies and kelpies. Why couldn't she come up with a better fib?

Idris said nothing but smiled as he exhaled a stream of smoke, politely directed away from Fina's face. Why was she still standing so close to him?

"Come," he said, touching her lightly on the arm. "I want to show you something."

"But shouldn't we get back to the other guests? Why are you here?"

"My, my. So inquisitive," he said, grinning again. It was a charming smile, she had to admit. "Well, if you must know, I had a bit too much time with the group. I wanted peace and quiet before I go back to our merry party."

"But couldn't you go around the villa since we were already all on the terrace?"

"I made my excuses for a – what is the quaint euphemism in English? A call of nature." He pointed toward the end of the corridor. "Let's take that door outside."

Fina trotted after him, not understanding why she decided to follow.

A wall of sea air hit Fina in the face so forcefully that she gasped for breath. But then she smiled, taking in deep gulps of air as if it were sustenance.

"Where are we going?" she said to Idris, who walked toward a pathway along the cliff. It was still twilight – the colour of his green jacket glowed like an emerald set off by the rich brown of the dirt pathway.

Idris came to an abrupt halt, nearly causing a collision. He pointed to a long island off in the distance, lit only by the occasional flash of a lighthouse.

"That's Tavolara. Or I ought to say, the Kingdom of Tavolara."

Fina nodded. "I read about it before we arrived in Sardinia. Mostly because I know the king went abroad and left his sister as regent, correct?"

"Yes, but after she died last year, Italian politicians seized it," he said. Then he spat as he said, "Mussolini."

Fina didn't know what to say or do, except to bob her head in sympathy. She changed the subject. "Is that what you wanted to show me?"

He shook his head and moved on without another word.

Soon they came upon a large beehive-like stone structure. She tilted her head back and peered all the way to the top. By the worn stones and general design, she realised this wasn't a modern structure.

Idris held both hands aloft as if he were conducting an orchestra. "Isn't it marvellous? It's a *nuraghi*. Native Sardinians built these all over the island almost 4,000 years ago."

In the gloam, Fina saw he was as excited as a small child. As if he felt the need to explain, he said, "As an architect, I have a great love of ancient buildings. It's incredible that these survived.I was going to wait to inspect it until tomorrow, but I couldn't wait any longer. Shall we take a look inside?"

"Don't you think the others are wondering where we are?" she asked, with a note of hopefulness in her voice. "Besides, we don't have a torch."

He smiled as he withdrew a small torch from his pocket.

Out of excuses, and not wanting to be a wet blanket, Fina toddled after Idris into the murky darkness. Fortunately, the torchlight was strong, but she had to stay close to him to see properly. The inside of the nuraghi smelt not unpleasant, much like the decaying soil smell of a nursery. Her shoes would be ruined though by the sticky muck layering the floor.

Something tickled the tops of her feet. And then was gone. Better not to speculate about it, she told herself.

Once they were inside, Idris shone the torch on the vaulted ceiling.

A rush of screeching and fluttering assaulted their senses. Wings flapped past them out of the small doorway.

As they grabbed each other involuntarily, Idris' torch slid from his fingers and rolled across the floor.

"What was that?" he gasped.

"We disturbed a nest of bats," said Fina, still gripping his arms. She couldn't let go. Neither, apparently, could he.

"You're shivering. And you have goose pimples," he said, removing his jacket and draping it over her. "It was thoughtless of me to take you out here in your dress."

Fina responded by moving toward the torch in the corner.

Though the open floor plan of the beehive structure meant there were no walls or other obstructions, the torch rolled behind a large object covered in canvas. She reached behind it, straining her fingers to grasp the torch.

"Blast it."

"What is it?" Idris hissed from behind her. Why were they whispering? He was very close now.

"My hand is stuck," she said, jerking her arm upwards.

"Just a moment," he said, lifting the canvas. In the dim light coming from the hidden torch, she spotted what appeared to be a machine.

He crouched down and dragged the machine by its feet. "At last!" Fina said as her arm sprung free. Idris took her arm and rubbed it gently.

"Are you injured?"

"Ah, no," she said, meeting his eyes and then looking down at his hand on her arm.

Not knowing what to do next, she scooped up the torch next to her.

"Is that a spinning wheel?" she asked, shining the torch on the machine.

"Looks to be a printing press," he said as he moved closer toward her. A strand of hair tickled the back of her neck as he inhaled and exhaled.

"That's odd," she said, "Why would you store such a thing in an ancient structure? And why would a shoe designer and a painter own a printing press?"

He shrugged, moving even closer. Fina took a step back but then halted.

They stood together in the darkness. Only a lonely cricket chirped somewhere outside. Idris grabbed her waist and pulled her in closer. For a long kiss.

12

"Where on earth have you been?" asked Ruby. "I was becoming concerned," she said, moving closer to Fina. Her eyes diverted toward Idris, who stepped out onto the terrace a minute after Fina. Fina didn't need a mirror to sense her face was scarlet, though hopefully a softer shade of scarlet given the darkness surrounding the pool.

"I see," said Ruby, giggling, and gave Fina a squeeze. Fina turned away.

Flashes of orange, white, red, green, black and yellow danced across Fina's vision. And they were dancing for a reason. Someone had turned up the Victrola and everyone, save Ruggero, Nefeli and Silvio, were dancing around the pool. It was a marvellous scene as couples spun around the perimeter of the pool. Fina was certain if she joined in she would be the first to fall into the pool.

The next song was a ballad. Zenash said, "Adriana, would you skip this one and put on something with a bit of fizz?"

Adriana grinned as she floated toward the Victrola. She certainly knew what fizz meant. The couples twirled with frenetic energy.

Nicola held out his hand to Ruby. She took it. He looked as happy as a cuckoo in the nest of its neighbour. Fina watched as Gina threw daggers in Ruby's direction. Ruby was unaware or undisturbed by this as she swayed onto the terrace-cum-dance floor.

"May I?" said Idris from behind her.

"You may," was all Fina could reply.

As they moved in formation around the perimeter of the pool, Fina said, "Why did you kiss me? Were you trying to stop me from asking questions?"

Splash.

As Fina had predicted, someone had fallen into the pool. How could they not? They were all dancing around a pool at night at a fast pace. And alcohol made one feel invincible.

It was Zenash. She sputtered in shock, flapping her arms up and down. Then she began to laugh and tread water.

"Do come in, the rest of you! It's delightfully warm!"

To Fina's utter amazement, she spotted Fabrizio's stocky figure run and leap into the pool. He scrunched himself into a little ball in mid-air. This had a spectacular effect. He created a tidal wave, spraying everyone within a few feet of the pool. Adriana shrugged as she wiped the water from her face. She was the next one to leap in, creating a look of a jellyfish floating on the surface. Soon everyone was laughing in the pool or standing awkwardly around the perimeter, staring at the swimmers.

Carlotta sneaked up in between Ruby and Fina, grabbed both of their hands and jumped into the pool. Fina felt her frock bubble up around her as she landed in the water. She tried to push it down, but it was no use. At least it was dark.

A frantic splashing noise came from her right. She paddled to the side of the pool and rested for a moment. Ruby had done the same. Ruby was a good sport, but she did not appear half pleased about Carlotta's invitation into the pool. The frantic splashing continued. Moving along the edge of the pool, hand over hand, she came closer to the noise. It was Fabrizio. His powerful arms flapped up and down, and she heard, rather than saw, the sounds of someone inhaling water.

"Help!" she cried. What was the word for help in Italian? "*Aiuto!*" "Someone help Fabrizio!"

Near one cluster of candles, she watched Silvio take a running jump into the pool. He took hold of Fabrizio – no easy task as he was still thrashing about – and dragged him to the side, where Renzo and Irene grabbed hold of either side of him and hoisted him over the edge of the pool. After he had coughed up a great deal of water, Fabrizio uttered a stream of invective in Italian.

By this time the guests had all climbed out of the pool. Zenash had a look of exhilaration. Carlotta's gurgled laughter sounded like a fish out of water. Idris had also jumped in – though Fina hadn't seen it – and was now patting his face dry with a cloth napkin. Adriana resembled a marble statue as her previous floating outfit was now wet and form-fitting. Ruby was the only one who looked genuinely distressed. Ruby did not enjoy these types of surprises.

Fina padded around the pool and gave Ruby a gentle side-hug. She whispered, "You were a good sport. But don't let it get you down. I have news I need to share." Fina realised she had to tell Ruby about the file, but she wasn't so sure she wanted to tell her about the Ian Clavering memo. She hadn't had a moment to read it yet, but it was safely tucked away in her handbag.

Ruby gave her a little thanks-for-being-a-friend-but-I'm-still-upset smile. But she said, "I want to hear all about your news in a moment."

The pair walked over to Renzo, who had stood up from his attendance over Fabrizio who was now sitting in a chair, muttering to himself.

"What happened?" asked Fina. "He obviously could swim – otherwise why would he jump in the pool?"

Renzo grimaced. "He says it was a ... oh, what do you call it?" he said, touching his calf.

"A leg cramp?" Ruby suggested.

Renzo held up his forefinger. "A cramp! What a delightfully expressive word for that pain."

Odd. As Fina glanced over at Fabrizio, he rubbed his neck rather than his leg. He rubbed it as if it were sore.

13

———

"I'm soaked," said Silvio, in the understatement of the year. He shook his head like a dog. Ruby and Fina moved away, avoiding the spray of water droplets.

Nefeli shivered, throwing on a wet wrap as if that would help keep out the cold. "Me too. And I've had a long day," she yawned. "I think I'll turn in."

Despite having jumped in the pool, Idris had managed to dry off more than the bystanders. He mimicked Nefeli's yawn, though, and said, "Good idea. I'll rest up so I'll have more energy tomorrow." Did he wink at Fina? Must be her imagination.

"We'll come too," said Ruby as she smoothed her hair.

As if their exodus had created more musical space in the air, Carlotta turned up the volume on the Victrola. Soon the air filled with whoops and laughter.

The bedraggled, wet crowd made their way slowly up the staircase, cautious not to slip on the marble steps. Fina watched Silvio enter the room with the goat painting. Nefeli padded into the room with the sheep painting. Her eyes lingered on Idris as he passed through the door with the wild cat painting. He didn't glance back at her.

Ruby and Fina gave a nod to each other which needed no verbalisation. They would change and meet in Fina's room.

After she had peeled off her wet clothes and put on a plush dressing gown, she plopped down in the upholstered chair near the window. In the rush of excitement, she had forgotten about the Ian Clavering memo. Ian Clavering, Ruby's old flame, as Fina now considered him, worked as an agent for someone. Not the British government, to be sure. But they didn't know any more than that. Still, Ian had warned them James Matua was watching them. They had learned little about why this was, but she suspected it was their continuing support of worker strikes in the Caribbean – which they hoped would spread elsewhere.

She knew Ruby would knock soon, so she ran to her handbag and retrieved the memo with Ian's name. She unfolded the wrinkled paper and scanned it rapidly.

Ian Clavering

BORN: *1910*
 Birthplace: Nassau, Bahamas
 Parents: Emerald Chester and Sidney Clavering
 Occupation: Theatre Producer

IAN CLAVERING HAS BEEN *a person of interest since 1933. While his occupation is a theatre producer, sources claim he also works for government or private interests. His primary task appears to be to pass information to various contacts and also to introduce contacts to one another. Most recently we have found possible connections to a Miss Ruby Dove, another person of interest.*

RECENT COMMUNICATIONS INDICATE INCREASED *importance of Clavering to possible interests allied against the British government. His exact role is unknown, but we recommend increased surveillance at this time.*

T.M.

SHE CRUMPLED up the piece of paper and stuffed it in her dressing gown. Fina swallowed, even though her parched throat made it painful – she was as thirsty as a dry riverbed. Now only if she had cocoa to quell her hunger and quench her thirst. Must be the drink and the saltwater, she thought, as she moved toward the water jug.

She spun round to see Ruby sitting in the chair by the door. Fina's hand flew to her neck. "You're sneaky, Ruby Dove!"

"Sorry. I thought it would make less noise if I just slipped in," said Ruby. She also wore a pink version of her blue dressing gown. How was it possible her hair still looked so perfect?

"Would you like some water?" said Fina, moving toward the water jug without waiting for a reply.

Ruby drained the glass in two seconds flat and held it out for more. After drinking three glasses in quick succession, she seemed ready to talk.

"I'm so exhausted, but I can't wait to hear what happened."

After Fina described her encounter with Nefeli, Ruby said, "So why does Renzo have these files – presumably not just about us, but others?"

Fina curled her legs underneath her to keep out the incipient chill. "What came to mind first was that he was a copper. But it makes little sense. So what, then? Is he someone like Ian?"

Ruby's eyes dilated. "Ian ..." said Ruby quietly. She stared out the window in an uncharacteristic gesture of daydreaming.

A stab of pain and worry shot through Fina's stomach. Ought she tell Ruby about the memo? She should, but later. Besides, Ruby wouldn't be able to sleep if she told her now.

"Well, I don't mean he's connected to Ian, but that he is an agent for someone," replied Fina.

"Surely not the British government."

"No, I agree it makes little sense. Could he be allied with the Italian Fascists?"

"Why would the Italian Fascists be interested in us? I doubt they'd even consider me capable of anything."

"And how wrong they'd be, Ruby Dove. But you're right, I cannot understand why they'd be interested."

Ruby rose and paced around the small rug in front of the door. "In his letter to me, Renzo said he wanted to discuss our activities. I had assumed he was one of us – most likely an anti-fascist of sorts, or maybe someone involved in an independence or labour cause. The fact that many of the guests here are exiles from Italian colonies makes it more likely he is against Mussolini."

"So perhaps the files are simply reports on our activities?"

"Could be. He said he wanted to meet with us tomorrow morning, so I suppose we'll find out more then," she said, stretching and yawning.

"But what about Nefeli? Do you think she'll tattle on me?"

Ruby shook her head. "I have the sense Miss Papas knows how to keep secrets." She paused. "And speaking of secrets," she said in a voice two octaves higher than before, "what were you doing with Idris?"

"He wanted to show me something ..." she mumbled.

"I bet he did!" she said, then threw back her head back and laughed.

14

———————

Light fingers of sun dappled Fina's face as she sat under an olive tree, sipping espresso.

Ruby lifted the floppy brim of her sun hat and winked at Fina. "This is the life, isn't it, Feens?"

She sliced a piece of cheese and pressed it into a slice of crusty bread. Then she popped the whole concoction in her mouth. "Mmmmhhh ..." she mumbled to Ruby as she chewed.

This terrace faced the inner harbour of Terranova Pausania. The houses, a smear of orange-pink, were interspersed with an occasional riotous green or red colour. Fina scanned her surroundings on Agrodolce and noticed the footpath they had ascended yesterday from the dock.

Pointing at the dock, she said to Ruby, "Deuced peculiar. The rowing boats have vanished. And I had assumed that's where Renzo docked his larger boat last night."

Ruby waved her hand in a gesture of dismissal or to rid herself of a persistent flying insect. "There must be another dock on the island. Or it's possible Ruggero went fishing this morning. He told me yesterday he was keen on fishing."

"Yes, but he wouldn't need three boats to go fishing."

The clatter of a dish next to them interrupted their conversation. Fabrizio pointed at the new plate of cheese he had brought to them. He pulled up a chair and began to share their breakfast, loading his plate with everything in sight.

"Is that yours, Fabrizio?" asked Ruby, looking down at a handkerchief. An irregular pattern of dark red speckled the front. Was it blood?

Fabrizio jumped like a hen on a griddle. He bent down and scooped up the handkerchief, quickly stuffing it his pocket. "*Scusi*," he said, eyes darting sideways. He jabbed a finger at his cheek and then made a motion back and forth.

"Shaving?" asked Ruby. Fabrizio nodded.

Before Fina could formulate a more detailed question in Italian about why he had no visible scars on his cheek, Zenash emerged from the ether. She wore an enormous, glamorous hat and a yellow floaty kaftan. After pouring herself espresso from the pot, she lit a cigarette. Holding it between two fingers, she gestured at Fina.

"Did you enjoy your swim last night?"

Fina noticed Ruby purse her lips and look out to sea.

Unsure of how she ought to answer this question, Fina said, "It was a new experience for me – swimming in a frock. I can cross that off my list of items I have to do in my life – and never need to do again."

Zenash chuckled. "Did you bring your bathing dress? I'm going in for a dip soon. Everyone ought to join me," she said, pausing before she moved her gaze to Fabrizio. "Except, of course, you, Fabrizio. No swimming for you?"

His head shook so vigorously Fina worried he might hurt his neck. Neck. She peered at his neck a little closer. It was red. She couldn't tell if it was sunburn. But it couldn't be sunburn – she saw blue–purple marks. He had rubbed his neck last night after his scare in the water. Perhaps he had somehow hurt himself?

Rummaging around in her handbag, Fina pulled out a bottle of aspirin. She offered it to Fabrizio. He waved his hand emphatically in what was clearly a gesture of rejection. Hmph. He could be a little more gracious about it. But then again, that was his nature.

Ruby wiped her fingers on a napkin. "I have a few letters I'd like to write, but you and Fina ought to enjoy yourselves in the pool," she said to Zenash.

After draining three espresso cups, Zenash stubbed out her cigarette. "Don't dawdle too long. The pool awaits!" she cried. And with that, she trotted at a gentle clip back to the villa.

Ruby and Fina followed close behind. Through a ground floor window, they watched Adriana painting a large watercolour on an easel. She was dressed in a painter's smock, covered in a riot of drips of colour. One paintbrush was gripped between her teeth, while another held her hair in an impromptu bun.

In the next window along, they spotted Renzo's back in a chair. He was running his hand through his hair between puffs on a cigarette the size of a stubby pencil.

As they entered the entrance hall, the smell of freshly cut eucalyptus hit Fina like a delicious, all-enveloping embrace. The guests who decided against breakfast *al fresco* were assembled here. Ruggero, Silvio, Nefeli and Irene sat together at a small table, picking at bread, cheese and fruit. They smiled and nodded at Fina.

As Ruby and Fina neared their bedroom doorways, Ruby said, "Sorry not to join you, Feens, but I want to prepare a few things before I talk to Renzo later. I need to sort out my thoughts."

"I understand. My head is fuzzy after last night, so I hope a dip might revive me."

After donning her green bathing dress, she grabbed a towel

and skipped down the hallway to the stairs. She wasn't used to walking on marble, so she was extra cautious on these stairs.

"Boo!" said Zenash, after tapping Fina on the back. Where did the woman get this much energy? She'd have to ask her what she ate. That must be it. Although Fina certainly couldn't survive on a breakfast of coffee and cigarettes. The thought of it made her queasy.

Towels draped over their shoulders, they padded toward the pool. The builders of the house had positioned it so the morning sun would hit the surface. Fina shivered slightly as she realised the water must have cooled down a great deal overnight. But she was here for an invigorating dip, wasn't she?

They slid off their sandals and dashed toward the pool. The tile surrounding it chilled Fina's toes.

Zenash made an expert dive. All Fina could manage was a jump, much like Fabrizio's plunge last night. She was about to leap when she stopped with her toes curled over the edge of the pool.

Zenash screamed. And screamed.

A tangerine, foamy dress floated gently in the water. Fina stared at a torso and legs draping below, creating the effect of an enormous, poisonous jellyfish.

Carlotta.

Fina screamed. She couldn't stop. Even as she opened her mouth, she couldn't believe it was happening. Someone grabbed her from behind. It was Nicola.

He squeezed her so tightly she couldn't breathe. She exchanged her screaming for choking.

"Nicola! What are you doing?" scolded a voice nearby. Gina. Of course. Gina must have thought he was taking advantage of Fina. Really, to think such a thing at a time like this.

Nicola released her and patted her hand. He turned to his wife, who had stuck out her lower lip and crossed her arms.

Fina could not bear to glance at the corner of the pool where Carlotta lay. By now, everyone had arrived. Ruby gave Fina a hug and draped her in a tablecloth.

"Why are you dressing me in a tablecloth, Ruby?"

"You're in shock, Feens. Besides, you're only in your bathing dress."

"I'm not in shock. I'm fine. I've seen plenty of dead bodies by now." And there it was. Those memories of her brother and father arose again. She doubled over from grief, though it probably appeared to be a stomach cramp. Ruby piloted her to a nearby lounge chair. She dashed into the villa and returned with a glass of brandy.

"Here. Drink this," she said, handing her the glass.

"No thank you, it's too early for me."

"Don't be obstinate, Fina Aubrey-Havelock. You know it's medicinal."

Fina did as she was told. The warmth of the brandy enveloped her, as did the intensifying sun.

Ruby sat down next to her. She leant over and whispered, "There's enough of a crowd over there; it won't help if I join them. I'll wait." Her eyes scanned the pool area. She pointed at a cluster of shrubs nearby. "See those? Notice anything?"

"They strike me as normal shrubs."

"But it looks like someone trod on them."

Silvio and Irene diverted them as they lifted Carlotta out of the water and onto the terrace. Carlotta resembled Ophelia – peaceful, serene, and just the same as she had looked last night.

Renzo bent over her, crying. The tears seemed genuine. Silvio whispered something to Renzo and then helped him up. The doctor leant over the body, waving everyone else away.

Everyone else milled about aimlessly. A few had followed Ruby's lead and now sipped brandy. Nefeli had knocked back a few glasses already. She was still steady on her feet, however. Must be a secret drinker, reflected Fina. And what about all those showy dresses in her suitcase?

Silvio stood up and touched his coiffed hair. Still not a strand out of place.

"*Scusi*, ladies and gentlemen. Would you please leave this

area? You may go wherever you like, but please stay away from the pool until we can find out what happened.

"Isn't it obvious?" asked Idris. "She drowned."

Silvio frowned. "I'm uncertain. I will need time to confirm. But be careful. I'm concerned the pool might be dangerous – perhaps there are loose tiles."

~

FINA RUBBED HER EYES. "Let's go for a walk. I'll feel cooped up in the house. I want to mull things over."

After Fina had dressed, the two of them slipped on walking sandals and descended the backstairs to avoid the pool. Ruby pointed to the pathway leading to the dock. "Remember how you noticed those boats were missing? Everyone was there at the pool a few minutes ago, so all the boats ought to be there. I asked Ruggero about it when I went for another cup of tea. He didn't have an explanation."

Glad of something to distract herself, Fina nodded. They took the steep steps down to the dock. It was a faster route than the dirt pathway. Another gloriously beautiful day, even though it was a terrible one. Fina marvelled at how the weather couldn't care less about human problems. Their arrival at the dock confirmed there was no transportation back to the mainland. Waves lapped against the dock as they inspected the posts where the ropes had been tied. What was odd – even odder than the missing boats themselves – was that there was still some rope attached. It could only mean one thing.

"Could there have been a storm last night? I slept like a top." Even as Fina uttered these words, she knew it was a ridiculous question.

"No, Feens. Someone cut the rope. Deliberately."

Fina pictured her own Adam's apple gliding down her throat. "Why would someone want to do that?"

Ruby patted Fina as if she were a cat who would not stop meowing. "Because someone doesn't want us to leave the island."

Fina sat down on the dock and let her legs drape over the side. She was distracted by the discovery of spiny urchins in the water. Their spikes waved ever so slowly as they glided toward their quarry: in this case, an unsuspecting mussel. Ruby remained standing. Rigid.

"But surely other boats can travel to the island," said Fina, pointing to the mainland which seemed to be rather close from this vantage point. "Besides, won't the ferry come again?"

Ruby shook her head and leant against one of the posts. She hugged it as if it would give her extra moral support. "I asked Ruggero about the ferries when I talked to him about the missing boats. He said they only run from Sunday morning to Friday morning. But the ferry doesn't come in close to the island, remember? You need a boat to row out to the ferry."

Fina stood up and brushed her hands together as if she had just completed a satisfying task. "A simple phone call can solve all of this. Renzo can call someone on the mainland and they'll fetch us."

"I'm afraid not, Feens. There's no phone on the island."

16

Fina's stomach grumbled. Breakfast had been hours ago. They had walked the perimeter of the island to ensure there weren't any hidden coves where the boats might be located. They found one beach with a small cave, but it was empty. Another dock sat on the opposite side of Agrodolce, but it too was empty. Besides, it was much too small for a boat. It was a stretch to even call it a dock. Ruggero had told Ruby it was his favourite place to fish. A broken pole by the dock confirmed his story.

"I'm ravenous. Can we return to the villa now?" pleaded Fina. "My feet hurt."

"Where's your adventurous spirit this morning, Feens?" Ruby's hand flew to her mouth as if it would stop her from talking. "I'm sorry. It's such a beautiful day that I forgot about your shock. But just remember it was an accident."

"Do you think so? I mean, was it an accident?"

Ruby's eyes widened. "Surely it wasn't suicide. That would be a silly way to try it. And as for murder, well, we're among friends! This isn't like our other cases where we've had to be on the lookout for someone nefarious. Everyone here is one of our own, or else not involved in politics."

Fina stopped and stared at her friend. "I'm surprised by you, Ruby Dove. I cannot believe that suspicious mind of yours has fallen asleep. There's something rather rum about this set-up. Besides, the boats being deliberately cut loose ought to be enough to make you consider foul play."

Ruby spun around from her position as leader on the trail. "I'm not sure ..." she trailed off as her scrunched-up face relaxed. "Perhaps I'm suffering from a bit of shock as well. I wanted to feel relaxed on this island because I felt I was among friends. No one has said anything rude to me, people have listened to me, and everyone has been hospitable." She paused. "You know how rare that is for me."

"Yes, you're quite right," Fina said, softening her tone. "Most everyone has been in high spirits – with the occasional human emotion thrown in. But we shouldn't let that lull us to sleep. We need to investigate further. And we're the best ones to do that, aren't we?" she said, with what she hoped was an encouraging smile.

"Dear Feens, what would I do without you?" Ruby rubbed her belly. "I'm peckish. But let's loop back to Adriana's artist's studio on our way to the villa. I want to take a quick look."

"Wait," said Fina, grabbing Ruby's arm. There would never be a perfect time to tell Ruby about the Ian Clavering memo. Now was as good a time as any, especially given Carlotta's death.

Ruby stared at Fina as if she had lost her marbles. "Jupiter's teeth! You're pinching me. What on earth is the matter?"

"Jupiter's teeth?" giggled Fina. She removed the crumpled memo from her pocket and thrust it at Ruby. She had taken to carrying it with her everywhere she went. Away from prying eyes.

Ruby read the memo, speaking the words out loud as if she couldn't comprehend their meaning. Her eyes flickered and then narrowed as her left hand balled into a fist. She took a deep breath.

"I need to let this marinate. It definitely means Renzo might have lured us here into a trap. But there's nothing we can do about it right now," she said, stuffing it back into her pocket.

"Ought we try to put it back into the file so Renzo doesn't notice it's missing?"

"I doubt he'll notice – at least for the time being. He's too distracted by Carlotta's death." Ruby stared out over the horizon. She turned toward Fina and said softly, "Thanks for taking care, as always, Feens."

Noticing Ruby's eyes were becoming glassy, Fina said, "Let's finish what we set out to do, as you suggested. Off to the studio!"

The studio roof popped up over the hill as they rounded a treacherous pathway. Ruby held up one finger as a silent warning.

Waves lapped against the shore. And a few birds squabbled on the rocks below.

Ruby waved Fina closer. Fina moved underneath the eaves of the studio.

She heard a stream of Italian invective. It sounded like Adriana.

Then a few staccato words fired in rapid response. Also in Italian. Must be Zenash.

Fina squeezed her eyes shut to block out all distractions.

"Bloody fool ..." said Adriana. "And those paintings!"

"Those shoes, well ..." said Zenash. She must have turned away because Fina couldn't hear the next few words. Then she said, "Carlotta had it coming ..."

And then everything went silent. Too silent. Had they heard them approaching?

Ruby took decisive action. She said in a loud, exaggerated voice, "Let's see if Adriana is in her studio, Fina!"

They thumped their feet to make plenty of noise.

Adriana emerged to greet them.

"Darlings. Did you enjoy your walk? It's the best thing to do after such a tragedy. Distract oneself. That's why I came to paint," she shook her head sadly. "Such a tragedy."

Fina was not buying her act. It seemed too forced. But maybe she felt she had to exaggerate her grief, especially as a host.

Zenash appeared behind Adriana. She pursed her lips in a line of grim agreement. "I was in such a state of shock, as I suppose you must have been, too," she said, turning toward Fina. She pressed her fingers over her eyes. "I have been trying to get that image out of my mind. I won't sleep well tonight ... poor Carlotta," she added hastily.

Ruby nodded solemnly as they had a moment of silence.

"We're on our way to the villa for lunch," said Ruby, glancing at her watch. "Would you care to join us?"

"Ah, lunch. Yes," said Zenash. "I'm afraid I'm not that hungry."

Fina felt a stab of guilt for being ravenous. But then she reminded herself that grief has different effects on the appetite.

"I don't have a proper appetite, either, but I desperately need an espresso," said Adriana.

They all trundled back to the villa, following the longer path around the back to avoid the pool.

Fabrizio met them at the rear entrance. "Lunch. Terrace," he announced, as if he were delivering bad news.

17

———

"If I may have your attention, *scusi*," said Silvio, rising from his chair as if he were about to offer a wedding toast.

Lunch, such as it was, was over. Idris patted his stomach. He had an appetite like Fina. He continued to avoid her, however. Ruggero had already irritated Fina with his incessant knuckle cracking. She inched her chair away from him at one-minute intervals, as if she could escape like a limpet sliding away from a starfish.

Ruby sat next to Irene, chatting about London. Fina could tell that despite their valiant efforts, neither of them was genuinely engaged in the conversation. Nefeli and Nicola sat together, whispering something about accounts. Gina sat next to Nicola, glaring at him as if discussions of finances were a prelude to something more romantically thrilling. Zenash, Renzo and Adriana sat together but said nothing to one another. Zenash folded a piece of paper into a bird and set it on the table. Its wings flapped in the whispering afternoon breeze.

Only Fabrizio was missing.

"Yes, *scusi*," repeated Silvio. "Renzo asked me to deliver the sad news. We all thought Carlotta's death was accidental—"

"Surely she didn't kill herself by drowning!" exclaimed Gina.

Nicola put a hand over Gina's. It wasn't a reassuring pat. It was to hold her back from saying more.

Renzo cut into the exchange. "She was murdered. Or I should say someone murdered her. Stabbed in the back."

Predictable gasps and hand-wringing ensued. Idris was the only one who didn't move a muscle in a display of shock or outrage.

Ruby held up her hand as if she had the answer to an important question in a primary school class. "Was the cause of death stabbing or drowning?"

Silvio's hair trembled like an oak losing its leaves in autumn. "What do you mean? How could the cause of death be drowning when she was stabbed?"

Ruby licked her lips and smoothed her hair. Fina used to consider these gestures as nervous habits but realised they were habits to buy her time when she felt irritated.

"Well, it's possible she drowned and then someone stabbed her," she said with a shrug.

"But why would someone stab her after drowning her?" asked Irene. "It makes little sense. They must have panicked after killing her and thrown her into the pool."

Renzo and Silvio nodded together as if that were the final word. Ruby's eyes narrowed as she gazed out to sea. Fina realised they weren't going to go much further in this enquiry – at least not in front of everyone.

"We must call the police," said Gina in a tone which suggested it was a fresh, brilliant idea. Everyone turned toward her. Fina observed that everyone's eyes narrowed or widened with distress. Well, well. For once, she and Ruby were in the majority in their disinclination to call the authorities.

Gina shrank back in her chair. Nicola had removed his hand from hers in a paroxysm of disgust.

Renzo gave Gina a wan smile as if she were a small child. "Even if I wanted to call the police, I'm afraid it's not a possibility. When the villa was built a few years ago, I decided not to have phone lines installed. Too expensive. And I wished to be left in peace."

Not one to give up, Gina carried on. "Well, we must do something. We cannot leave her by the pool. And I, for one, want to go back to the mainland." She turned to Renzo. "Not that you haven't been a delightful host, of course, but this puts a damper on a weekend party."

Renzo removed his sunglasses. His eyes were red and puckered. He must have really cared for Carlotta.

"Ruby and I confirmed we are marooned. The three boats were set adrift sometime yesterday or last night. Someone cut the ropes that moored them to the dock," said Fina.

This time, instead of verbal reactions, Fina noticed the body language of fear. Everyone became still and rigid.

Nicola spluttered, "But ... but ... Renzo, you must have another boat, or another way to communicate. What about the ferry?"

A flash of purple flew before Fina's eyes. It was Adriana. She wore a similar concoction as yesterday, though this time it was in a deep royal purple. She flew at Renzo. "I told you inviting that woman here was a disastrous idea! But did you listen? No. What a silly man you are. And now we're in this mess," she said.

Renzo's eyes flashed. "It was your idea to have a weekend party! To have all of these artists here. You said it would be divine. So I did my best to find the finest creative guests I could. Carlotta is one of the most creative people I know. Or knew," he finished, his voice lowering.

Idris rose from his seat and said, "It's no good blaming each other. Neither of you – at least I believe this – committed this murder, so how could you possibly anticipate the weekend would come to this?"

Adriana and Renzo's tensed muscles relaxed. Both slumped down into nearby chairs.

Apparently seeing an opportunity to carry on, Idris said, "We will be on this island for the foreseeable future. One of us is a murderer."

Zenash said, "It could have been someone who came to the island in the middle of the night and killed Carlotta. Then they made their escape and set the boats loose as well."

"Yes – that has to be it!" said Nefeli, moving her fingers into a steeple alignment. "Someone had a grudge against Carlotta, so they came here, stabbed her, threw her in the pool and then cut off all of the boats. That way, they'd have time to escape before the police began to search for them!"

Renzo let out a long stream of cigarette smoke up into the air as he stuck out his lower lip. "That would be a convenient explanation. Except no one – save us – knew Carlotta was on this island."

"What my foolish brother is trying to say is he invited her for a liaison this weekend," said Adriana, grinning maliciously.

Gina scowled. Zenash swung one of her crossed legs. Nicola slicked back his hair.

Renzo grimaced at the word "foolish," but nodded slowly. "We were having an affair. I see no point in denying it. She made sure not to tell anyone she was coming here. I believe she told her husband, though I doubt he listened or cared, that she would visit a girlfriend in Milan."

Ruby returned to an earlier theme. "What if her husband found out somehow and came here in a jealous rage?"

Renzo chuckled. Not in a jovial way, but the way one does when everything looks so awful you have to laugh. "Her husband, well, was not interested. Not in her and not in any women at all. Carlotta told me they had agreed a few years ago to live separate lives. He wouldn't have cared enough to kill her, much less plan this elaborate attack."

"Isn't her husband a fascist?" asked Nicola in a hushed tone.

Adriana nodded. "He is a major supplier of arms to Mussolini's government. He uses his business connections to facilitate the transactions. Most of the funds come out of his own pocket."

"And Carlotta?" asked Ruby, rejoining the conversation.

"Carlotta was as apolitical as anyone I've ever met. Which is a complex feat during these times," said Renzo.

Everyone's heads nodded in gentle agreement.

"Well, this brings us back to my original point," said Idris, sighing. "One of us is a murderer."

18

Irene cleared her throat. "How many of us have had any detecting experience?"

Everyone raised their hands except for Ruggero, Fabrizio and Gina.

Fina almost fell out of her chair. She noticed similar movements among the other guests.

Irene's eyes widened. "How is it possible?"

"Why don't we all explain what we mean by detecting?" suggested Adriana.

One by one, each guest explained their sleuthing experiences.

"I detect diseases," said Silvio, solemnly. Fina could never tell when Silvio was joking or serious.

"Adriana and I solved a mystery of the embezzled accounts a few years ago, didn't we?" said Renzo, looking at his sister. Her eyes widened. "We did indeed, but it was too late to save the money, unfortunately."

"Well, I suppose part of my profession is detecting," said Irene. "I spot forgeries."

"If we're considering crimes that are not as serious as

murder, then I also qualify," said Idris. "I know who has been supporting Italian incursions into Libya."

"Will you tell us?" asked Ruby.

He shook his head. "No, but I am rather proud of my own deductions in that area. Let's say I have confirmation that I am correct."

"We had a shoe thief, didn't we darling?" said Nicola to Gina. "And I soon found the culprit. Unfortunately, the thief was an employee."

"I'm not sure you'd call it detecting," said Zenash, waving a cigarette. "But I have an ability to know when famous people are not where they're supposed to be. That's why I enjoy celebrity gossip. It confirms what I already know." She shot a look at Renzo. Was the look about Carlotta's trip to Sardinia when she told her husband she was going to be elsewhere that weekend?

"Accounting is detecting," said Nefeli, tucking a wisp of hair behind her ear. "And like Adriana and Renzo, I have found many irregularities over the years. At least five serious embezzlers."

"Did you go to the police?" asked Nicola.

"No," replied Nefeli with venom. "I avoid them at all costs. We came to some understandings about the accounts each time. Besides, these were not my accounts, so all I could do was make suggestions to the owners about how they wanted to pursue justice."

Justice. Nefeli's last comment cast a layer of tension over the gathering. Ironically, Ruby broke it with their Caribbean murder story.

"Fina and I took a cruise – for work – a few months ago in the Caribbean. There were a few murders on that journey and a limited number of suspects – much like the scenario we're in right now," said Ruby. A number of people shifted in their seats at this comment.

"Ruby's detecting skills were so strong the murderer pursued her, believing she would reveal all before the ship arrived in Port of Spain," added Fina. She fell silent. That wouldn't give the murderer ideas, would it? No, she told herself, the murderer wouldn't need any prompting from her if they suspected any one of the guests knew anything at all.

Adriana bit her lip. "I suppose the best plan of action is to ask everyone who has had detecting experience to, well, detect."

Ruby and Fina stared at each other, still in disbelief. How was this possible?

Idris said, "So you mean we all ask each other questions and do a bit of sleuthing on our own? Isn't that a little dangerous?"

Ruby replied, "I agree the idea is crackers, but if we were to follow it, I'd suggest we split into pairs. That way, if one person is paired with the murderer," she said, shivering despite the warm breeze, "the murderer won't dare to murder their own partner."

Adriana smiled with approval. "*Fantastico*. Let us begin."

"But wait!" said Gina. "Before we begin this game, tell us, Renzo, are we stuck here forever?"

"No, dear Gina. Workmen travel from the mainland every month to work on repairs. They'll arrive on Tuesday."

Gina let out a sigh somewhere between relief and frustration. She waved her hand at Adriana. "Do carry on."

Adriana clapped her hands. She was warming to this idea. "How should we pair up?"

Fabrizio stood up and removed a matchbook from his back pocket.

He tore out the matches, one by one.

Adriana glanced over and nodded approval. "*Bene*. Fabrizio will make matches of different lengths. You must match up your matches – ah, what a delightful language English is – to find your partner."

"Are there other rules?" asked Nicola.

"Does everyone take part, including Ruggero, Fabrizio and me?" asked Gina.

"Why not?" said Adriana. "It only makes sense that everyone gets involved. As for rules, there aren't any, except you shouldn't get too carried away. This isn't a game."

Fabrizio held up his large hand in triumph. It was lined with matches which all appeared to be the same height, but weren't, of course. He tramped over to each guest as if he were offering them a special delicacy of their choosing. After everyone had drawn their lot, a comic scene ensued as everyone tried to find their partner.

"Ah! Irene! I'm so glad I selected you," said Idris.

Gina glared sourly at her husband as he and Adriana held up their matching matches in triumph. Gina found herself paired with Ruggero. She rolled her eyes.

Zenash and Ruby. Renzo and Nefeli. Silvio and Fabrizio.

"Did we miscount?" asked Ruby.

Adriana's mouth formed into a large O. "Oh, *scusi*, I am so sorry, Fina. I was thinking of the list for dinner. And that included poor Carlotta."

Now the centre of attention, Fina felt the same way she had in the school playground when she was the last person selected for a team sport.

Ruby stared at Fina with a look of distress. "Let's have a trio. Fabrizio – take a match from each pair and let Fina select one."

Fabrizio sprang into action. Fina closed her eyes and removed a match from his sweaty hand.

"It's the shortest," she said, holding it aloft.

"That's us," said Irene and Idris in unison. Fina smiled. She liked both of these people. Especially one of them. Surely neither of them was the murderer.

~

RUBY WIPED her grandmother's blue handkerchief across her forehead. "Whew. Well, this an unusual addition to our fast-growing list of adventures. Never had to play detective against detective. Except with the police of course, but that's a different kettle of fish."

Fina sucked on a slice of orange. She usually ate the whole slice, but oranges were so plentiful she felt like she could just enjoy the juice. Except now she had strands of orange caught between her teeth.

"Yes. This is new for us. And even more so since we're not sleuthing together in our team of Dove & Aubrey-Havelock."

"Sounds like a solicitor's firm," Ruby laughed.

"What do you think of Zenash?" asked Fina as she grabbed another slice of orange.

Ruby swayed in the rocking chair near the window. "Obviously I am a devotee of her and her books. So I am prejudiced. But I genuinely like her, regardless of her status as a writer."

"Could she have done it?"

She stopped rocking and put her feet firmly on the floor. As if it would help her think more clearly. "Well, it's early days, as they say. We have no idea about murder, motive or opportunity. Could she be a murderer? Yes. It's possible. But despite her warm, open and emotive personality, she wouldn't kill – at least not without a lot of planning."

"Hmmm ..." said Fina, wiping her sticky fingers on a hand-kerchief. "I agree with you, but why did she and Idris pretend not to be acquainted with one another that first day at the hotel? Something struck me as odd about the conversation at the time. Were they trying to fool Nefeli?"

"Perhaps they didn't trust her at first. Maybe it's a habit of both Idris and Zenash. After all, they both experienced traumas which would make them wary of trusting anyone."

"That's plausible," said Fina, blowing at her fringe. "Back to the point about planning, though. We don't know everyone well yet, but I'd say the impulsive murderer crowd includes Gina and Fabrizio."

"And possibly Adriana," added Ruby. "Though she's cheeky and smart enough that I imagine her doing it either way."

Ruby stretched her arms out and massaged her neck.

"Something amiss with your neck?" asked Fina.

"It must have been those pillows. They're different shapes to what I'm used to. Don't worry – it will go away with a little massage," she said, pausing as she craned her neck from one side to another. "What do you think about your partners?"

Fina rested her head against the headboard and stared at the ceiling. Like almost everything else in the villa, the ceiling displayed close attention to detail. She guessed Adriana had painted the mosaic-like pattern.

"I suppose Idris strikes me as too cool."

"Sounds like I describe him as too hot," giggled Ruby.

Fina threw a pillow.

"Ahem," she said in mock seriousness. "There's something off, as if he's holding something back. And I don't understand why he's avoiding me."

"Probably because he likes you too much and is confused," said Ruby.

"As for Irene," said Fina, forging ahead. "She strikes me as someone who lives her life and doesn't care much for conventions. There's a certain rigidity underneath the skin that seems to be holding emotion – or a secret – in place. Still, neither are likely candidates."

"It will certainly be odd to be sleuthing without you," said Ruby sadly. "But it gives us double the chance to investigate and find more clues."

Fina peered at her watch with alarm. "I'm supposed to meet Idris and Irene in ten minutes downstairs."

Ruby mirrored her movement, eyeing her own watch. "And I'm meant to meet Zenash."

"Psst ..." said Fina as she closed the door to her bedroom. "Look," she said to Ruby, pointing to white specks on the floor.

Ruby bent down, but not before glancing around the corridor.

"Are they little bits of paper?" suggested Fina.

"Hmmm ... they're too tiny to be from a shredded note."

"I agree. They're almost like dust."

Ruby tapped her teeth. "Reminds me of decaying paper. Perhaps from a stack of old files?"

Fina nodded. "That must be it. Sorry for the distraction – let's meet our sleuthing partners downstairs!"

19

The entrance hall was deserted.

Ruby and Fina huddled together.

"Where is everyone?" asked Fina, rather inanely given the fact it was obvious no one was there.

A heavy shuffling sound emanated from somewhere below the ground floor.

Fabrizio emerged from the bowels of the villa. His hands were blotched with a red–purplish stain.

"Ah, *senore* ..." Fina began. She stopped, not because she couldn't find the vocabulary to carry on, but because she was at a loss for words.

He grunted and wagged his hand downward.

Ruby shrugged and toddled off after him as he began the descent back downstairs. Fina followed so closely a sharp stab of pain hit her ribs as Ruby jerked her elbow behind her.

They made their way down a stone spiral staircase into a cellar. Fina's hair brushed past the stone and became caught on a nubby outcropping. The low ceiling forced Ruby to crane her neck to the side. Fina breathed in deeply through her nose, but all she smelt was decaying earth wafting from below. She grabbed Ruby's arm in a vice grip.

"Feens! You're hurting me," hissed Ruby.

Fina relaxed her grip.

Finally, an anaemic light filtered up from the bottom of the stairs.

A welcome soft glow followed a clicking noise as Fabrizio flipped a switch in the corner of the cellar.

Ruby and Fina squealed in surprise. An enormous vat filled with almost-black grapes stood in the centre of the room. Dusty wine bottles lined the walls. Some half-turned away in shame, while others proudly displayed their label in red and white.

Fabrizio motioned to them to step into the vat.

Fina pointed to her skirt and feet with the hope it would convey her reluctance to soil her clothes.

Fabrizio knocked on his own head. Then he smiled and pointed to two faded black frocks hanging on the wall. He pantomimed turning around and covering his eyes, which he then proceeded to do.

The thrill of making wine was overshadowed by the half-terror Fina felt being in a dark cellar, with a murderer on the loose. But she didn't have time to ruminate as Ruby had already changed into one of the black frocks. Fina followed suit.

Ruby tapped Fabrizio on the shoulder. He spun round and pointed to an ancient rusty pail in the corner filled with water, and a stained mat underneath. They duly washed and dried their feet.

Ruby rushed up the steps to the vat, but Fabrizio dampened her enthusiasm with a *"stai calmo."* With an enormous Cheshire cat grin on her face, she leapt into the grapes.

"I've always wanted to do this, Feens! I had no idea Renzo made wine as well as shoes."

Fina legs tensed and wobbled as she ascended the stairs to

the vat. She lowered one leg into the vat and wriggled her toes as the cool, slimy mixture rose to her knee.

Fabrizio put his hands on his hips and hopped around the small, patterned rug on the floor, kicking his feet back in slow motion. Ruby followed, dancing her way methodically around the perimeter of the vat. She made smaller and smaller circles as she came closer to the middle. Naturally, she was methodical about the whole thing, even though the look on her face was one of spontaneous joy.

Fina gripped one hand on the vat and made slow, tentative motions with her feet.

"Come on, Feens, put your back into it!" cried Ruby as she twirled around. Fina's feet began to lift and press more rapidly. She heard a chuckle. Fabrizio was laughing at them. Fina had a good mind to pick up the slop and throw it at him. Instead, she scooped up a whole grape that had escaped the macerating motion of their feet and hurled it at his chest. It ricocheted into the darkness.

His wide eyelids crinkled as he let out a great belly laugh. Soon they were all laughing giddily as Ruby and Fina waddled around like ducklings in their first rain.

Quick and light footsteps came from the stairway.

The bent head with Renzo's lion mane peeked out first from around the bend in the stairs. As he lifted his head, Fina caught a flicker of utter surprise and delight, coupled with extreme frustration and relief.

"There you are! We've been searching everywhere for the three of you!" he said wiping his brow with a red handkerchief.

"Come. Your sleuthing partners are waiting for you."

Exhilarated from their delightful exercise, Fina noticed that they were the only ones with smiles on their faces when they entered the entrance hall.

Suddenly she felt like a small child who had disappointed

the adults. No matter – all rules could be broken when tracking down a murderer.

Irene was tapping her now purple-toed feet. Idris paced in front of the window. He gave Fina a rapid sidelong glance. She looked away.

Zenash sat on a windowsill ledge, smoking and peering longingly out the window. As soon as she saw Ruby and Fina enter, she hopped down from the ledge and glided toward Ruby.

Fina couldn't make out what the two were whispering. A sharp pain of jealousy pierced her stomach.

As if Ruby sensed Fina's discomfort, she cupped her hand in and whispered into her ear. "Don't worry, Feens. I won't let her celebrity overwhelm my grey cells. You know me. Always on guard."

Zenash waved her cigarette at the crowd. "Ruby and I will speak to Fabrizio and Silvio," she said in an artificial voice. Why was Zenash as jittery as a cat on hot bricks?

20

———————

Silvio's hair quivered as he pulled over two wicker chairs for Zenash and Ruby. Ruby smoothed her hair and skirt before sitting down. Zenash plopped down without any clothes adjustment. Ruby leant forward, while Zenash sat back, throwing one arm over the side of the chair.

Fabrizio, already seated at the round table, folded his hands across his solid stomach. He slapped his body occasionally, presumably to punish a mosquito in search of food.

"Let us begin," said Zenash as Silvio took his seat. He leant to one side, as if shifting his weight in the other direction might cause him and the chair to tumble off the cliff.

Silvio stared at Ruby. "Would you like to begin, my dear?"

"I'm not your dear, but I will begin. Renzo invited me to learn more about his shoe design business. Fina is an assistant and close friend, so he invited her as well."

Before Ruby could say anything further, Zenash intervened. "Why were you invited here this weekend?" she asked, gazing at Silvio. Then she answered her own question. "I first met Renzo at a show of mine in London. We became friends. He invited me because his sister is a painter and because he said he wanted to host an artist's weekend," she said, crossing and uncrossing her legs.

"You already know why I'm here. I'm Renzo's personal physician," said Silvio.

"Did you ever meet Carlotta before this weekend?" asked Zenash.

"Because Renzo has hired me as his personal physician, I have met Carlotta a few times."

"How long have you been Renzo's physician?" asked Ruby.

"About a year."

"And why does Renzo need extensive medical treatment? He seems to be the picture of health," said Zenash. Ruby gave Zenash an admiring gaze.

Silvio shifted in his seat and rubbed the side of his nose with one finger. "I'm not sure why this applies to what happened to Carlotta," he said.

"We won't understand why until we receive an answer," Zenash said.

"Well, I can say he suffers from bouts of melancholy and neurotic behaviour. The technical term is neurasthenia," he said, halting between each word of the sentence, as if it were being forced out of his mouth. "It's normally treated with electric therapy, though I am dubious about its efficacy."

Ruby shuddered. She recalled stories of women subjected to so-called electrotherapy. "Wouldn't he need to visit a psychiatrist?"

Silvio shook his head. "It's all interconnected for Renzo. He first came to me about various minor physical ailments. I told him his mood must be involved." He paused. "Renzo had some childhood experiences that make him, well, susceptible. We do talk about those experiences, though I am not a trained psychiatrist. He likes my approach."

"Does he take many pills or tonics?" gambled Ruby.

"Really, Miss Dove. That is confidential information."

"I see by your distress that he must take a great many pills," said Zenash, with a slightly malicious grin.

The only response was Silvio's shaking hair. He rose and wailed like a small child. He clapped one hand over his neck.

"Crikey! Are you all right?" asked Ruby.

Silvio swayed as he stood up. Ruby rushed over to steady him, despite the fact she might also suffer another bout of vertigo.

He pushed her away. "I've been stung by a wasp!" he screeched. Without waiting for a reply, he dashed toward the house.

Zenash was apparently unperturbed by this turn of events. She turned to Fabrizio and unfurled a stream of Italian. He answered leisurely and deliberately. Zenash leant over to Ruby and said, "He has worked for Renzo and Adriana for a while. Originally from Naples."

"So none of us had met Carlotta before this weekend, had we?" asked Zenash, who then translated the question into Italian for Fabrizio.

Ruby shook her head.

Fabrizio shook his head.

"Does Fabrizio suspect anyone?" asked Ruby.

Zenash translated the question. "He says he suspects Silvio. He says he doesn't trust anyone with hair so perfectly manicured," she laughed.

"If hair is his criteria, ask him about Nicola. His hair is perfect – most of the time," said Ruby.

"He claims he doesn't trust Nicola either. But mostly because he has a roving eye for the ladies."

Fabrizio grabbed Zenash's arm and pulled her closer. He whispered something into her ear.

Zenash sat up and said to Ruby, "He says we should watch Irene."

"Why?"

"She's been acting suspiciously. Coming back and forth to the cellar – always saying she's bringing wine, but sometimes she comes up empty-handed."

"Did Fabrizio confront her about it?"

Zenash leant over to Fabrizio. Then she said, "She just waves a dismissive hand at him and doesn't reply."

A loud foghorn pierced the silence.

21

———————

"Now you're here, we thought we'd speak to Adriana and Nicola. They're at the beach near the dock," said Irene to Fina.

The trio set off down toward the dock. Idris clasped his hands behind his back and moved with purpose along the cliff pathway. Irene's head spun round like a top – Fina was afraid Irene might trip if she didn't occasionally look down at those purple toes.

Fina tapped Idris on his shoulder, though she was reluctant to disrupt contemplation. "What are we going to ask them?"

He shrugged. "I like to let suspects ramble. Eventually, they reveal something important – even if it's not related to the murder – if they keep talking. It's what I always do with people who hire me to design their homes or offices. Though it's often awkward to sit in silence, I find it's better to let them spill out their hopes and dreams first. Then I can use that to better explain how I envision the design."

"I agree with you. A fly will not buzz into a closed mouth. Besides, since we know so little, I haven't a clue about what to ask."

She peered at him. His eyes wandered off into the distance. Hmph. So much for a light romantic interlude.

The small beach resembled a smear of butter against a piece of brown bread. Adriana and Nicola sat on makeshift lounge chairs, chatting casually. They didn't seem too bothered by their investigative tasks. Adriana wore another gauzy concoction, this time in azure. Nicola appeared ready to jump into the blue any minute in his bathing costume. Irene brought a stack of large towels with her which she flapped onto the sand as if she were making a bed.

Irene set out the towels in a small semi-circle around Adriana and Nicola's chairs. Though they were at a clear disadvantage sitting on the sand. Idris and Irene approached sitting down rather awkwardly, in the way cats circle three times before finding the right position for their afternoon nap. Fina, on the other hand, plopped down on the towel and immediately removed her sandals. Her toes wriggled as they dug farther and farther into the sand.

After Idris and Irene had finally settled down, Adriana bypassed all pleasantries and dove straight into the heart of the matter. "As we're all detectives, let's review our movements last night and early this morning."

"But wasn't she killed last night? Why account for our movements this morning?" asked Irene. "After all, she had on that orange dress she was wearing last night. She'd scarcely wear it to bed and then get up this morning in it."

Nicola nodded. "Irene is most correct."

"While you're right about the dress, the murderer could have killed her last night, but only pushed her into the pool this morning," said Fina.

Everyone stared at Fina – at least it seemed that way to her. It was challenging to tell with sunglasses looking back at her.

Idris cleared his throat. "Fina is right. It won't hurt to review everything. We have nothing but time," he said, gazing at the limitless expanse of the sea.

"I'll begin," said Nicola, patting down his hair. He had supplied his hair with more cream this morning, but it was already wearing off. "For those of you who stayed up after the jaunt in the pool, you know I was one of the last ones to retire for the night. Gina had already gone up to bed before that, so I was careful not to wake her. This morning, I awoke early – by habit – at 6 o'clock. I strolled around the island for about an hour, bathed, pottered about in my room and then came down to breakfast."

"And Gina? Where was she during all of this?" asked Irene.

"As I said, she was asleep when I turned in for the night. She was still asleep this morning when I left for my walk. When I returned to the room after my stroll, she was gone. I haven't asked her where she was during that time."

"What route did you take this morning for your walk? Wouldn't you have walked past the pool?" asked Fina.

Nicola shifted in his chair. "I left through the front door, so no. I took the path that passed the art studio."

He stopped and rubbed his chin. "That's peculiar," he said to himself. "It hadn't occurred to me until I said it aloud, but there was something odd about the studio," he said leaning back and staring at the sky as if it would provide the answer.

"Was the door open?" prompted Adriana.

Nicola shook his head.

"Could you see something – or someone – through the window?" asked Fina, warming to the guessing game.

He shook his head again and threw up his hands. Then he slapped his thighs in resignation. "It will come to me, but not now," he said, pausing. "To carry on, I walked past the studio, over to the dock at the other end of the island and then returned via the pathway which does, indeed, take one past the pool."

"And?" said Irene, drumming her fingers on the sand.

"And nothing. Nothing at all. You see, a difficult business matter occupied my thoughts, so I'm afraid I was not a keen observer of anything. Carlotta could have been in the pool and I wouldn't have necessarily noticed. But it's also possible she wasn't there at that time, either."

"This was at seven o'clock, correct?" asked Fina, scribbling in a small notebook she had surreptitiously withdrawn from her satchel. Adriana peered venomously – or was it jealousy? – at her notebook.

Nicola smiled at her as affirmation. He was charming and handsome. Fina wondered if she would be as jealous as Gina of a husband like that. Possibly, but she doubted it. Too much emotional energy – Fina spent most of her emotional energy on navigating anxiety.

Adriana removed her sunglasses and rubbed them with a red handkerchief. She half squinted at Fina in the sun, creating a grinning effect. "And you, Fina. Why don't you tell us your movements last night?"

She snapped her notebook shut and tapped her pencil against her lips. Had she acquired this habit from Ruby? "You all saw me in the pool. The same as Ruby. After we crawled out of the pool, we immediately went upstairs to change and get into bed."

"Did you two speak before going to bed?" asked Irene perceptively.

"After we changed, we talked about the events of the night. But nothing important," she said, hoping her unwavering voice was convincing enough. "Then, this morning, I rose at about half-past seven, went to bathe and then had breakfast on the terrace. Zenash suggested a swim, so I changed into my swimming costume. Ruby said she would write correspondence in her room instead, so Zenash and I went to the pool. You know the rest."

The waves crashing against the shore grew in size. A low, rumbling sound echoed in the distance. Everyone turned to look.

22

It was only a frigate, not too far off in the distance. The blue of the boat mirrored that of the sea, creating the illusion of a monster rising from the depths of the ocean. Everyone held their breath, as if the blue creature would come and rescue them. Oblivious to their plight, the boat chugged on and soon disappeared from view. But the wake remained.

The sun had disappeared behind a bank of puffy clouds. Was that a thunderhead? Fina shivered.

Idris pulled his towel over his shoulders. "How about we walk and talk?" he suggested. "I'm getting a chill."

They all agreed to walk to the small dock at the other end of the island. As they made their way up the steep hill, Fina turned as she heard a scream. Irene. She lay on an outcrop of the pathway up the hill, holding her ankle. Her face was so contorted she was almost unrecognisable.

"Fetch Silvio!" said Idris, running toward Irene. "Now!" he yelled at Nicola. Nicola shook himself and dashed off toward the villa. Adriana followed Nicola, though at a more leisurely pace.

"Does it hurt to touch it?" asked Idris, pointing at Irene's ankle.

She winced and nodded. "I'm sure it's nothing. I probably twisted it."

"Do you want to try to walk? We can help you back to the villa if we carry you, one on each side," he said with great concern.

She leant on Idris' arm for support and gradually made her way upright. She winced as she limped. "I'll be all right."

Peering over her shoulder, first to her right and then to her left, Irene whispered, "Let's inspect the studio. I want to search for the weapon."

Idris looked at Fina. Fina looked at Idris. "How about we search and you stay here? You shouldn't walk on that ankle. And you shouldn't be alone."

Irene opened her mouth and then closed it like a fish. "You're right, but be quick. I'll be fine. They'll be back soon."

Fortunately for Fina and Idris, the studio was nearby. Much closer than the villa.

The door was ajar, and creaked ominously as they pushed it open.

"Ruggero! What are you doing here?"

Ruggero spun round on his heel, nearly knocking over an easel. "Silvio said he wanted to be alone. I assume he thinks better on his own. Or perhaps he wants to write prescriptions or whatever it is doctors do in their spare time. So I thought I'd do a bit of sleuthing myself," he said sheepishly.

"Dangerous to be on your own," said Idris.

"I can take care of myself," said Ruggero huffily.

Selkies and kelpies. The masculine ego strikes again.

Fina scanned the studio. It looked much the same as it had the day before. The canvas on the easel had been covered, however.

Ruggero held out a welcoming hand. "I'd welcome the help," he said.

"What are you doing?"

"Searching. I've just started."

Without another word, Fina and Idris went to work, opening drawers and peering behind a stack of books on the bookshelf. Fina then concentrated on the artists' tools section. She opened a paintbox to reveal a set of well-worn watercolours. A drawer nearby revealed a sketch pad, pencil, pen and book of matches.

A vase full of paintbrushes tipped with reds, yellows, purples and blues reminded her of a cheerful flower arrangement. A flash of silver caught her eye. It wasn't a paintbrush.

"Idris and Ruggero!" Fina hissed. "Come here!"

The pair dutifully padded over to Fina's frozen position in front of the vase. Pointing at the case, she said, "There's a knife or dagger in there. Ought we touch it?"

Ruggero's eyes darted around the artist's set-up. They alighted on a rag near the easel. He scooped up the rag and rooted around in the mass of paintbrushes. Finding his quarry, he held a small dagger aloft. Its long, thin blade ended in a stubby wooden handle.

"Is it a letter opener?" asked Fina, coming closer to peer at it.

She jumped back. The left corner of Ruggero's mouth lifted in a smile.

Fina gulped as she felt goose pimples rise on her arm. Though she was with Idris, it was foolish to leave the relative safety of the larger group, enclosed and far away from the villa.

"There you are!" exclaimed Ruby as she traipsed in through the door.

She began to remove her sunglasses but stopped like a bone-dry steam train in the doorway.

"Ruggero," she said quietly. "What are you doing with that knife?"

No one moved.

"I-I just picked it up. She told me it was here!" he said as he pointed the knife at Fina.

Fina, Idris and Ruby held up their arms in a surrender position.

The knife clattered to the floor.

As if shaken from a dream, Ruggero bent over to retrieve the weapon and handed it promptly, encased in the artist's rag, to Ruby.

"I need air," he said, pushing past Ruby out of the studio.

"What in heaven's name was going on?" whispered Ruby.

Fina leant back against the wall for support. "It was as if he was possessed by the knife."

"You don't think he would do anything with it, do you?" Ruby enquired.

Fina bit her lip. "No, I was frightened – mostly because of the way he smiled – but I doubt he had any ill intent at all. It was as if he had been carried back to a moment in the past."

"It's better if we clear this up right now before the others arrive," said Idris.

"Why are you here, by the way?" asked Idris, glancing at Ruby.

"I found out about Irene's injury and came to help. When I noticed you two weren't there, I told the others I'd see if you were in the studio," she said, walking out of the gloom of the studio into the bright sunlight.

Ruggero stood near the doorway. His hands clasped in a tight ball.

"I owe you an explanation," he said, letting his hands fall to his sides, "about what happened in there. I'm sure you think I had something to do with the murder. But I did not – at least not directly. I've had many violent experiences in my life. When I saw the knife, it was as if I was in that moment in the past."

"When you murdered someone?" blurted Fina.

Ruby shot her a warning glare.

He frowned. "No, no. It wasn't that. I had discovered someone else's body."

"Why were you smiling, then?" queried Idris, arms crossed.

"Was I? How odd. As I told you, I was in that moment, so I'm afraid I didn't understand what I was doing," he said. He put a hand on Ruby's arm. "You must believe me. It has nothing to do with the tragedy here," he said softly.

Ruby's mouth was set in a straight line. "If it were a tragedy, why were you smiling?"

"I've been told that I smile when I'm lost in thought. I know it's an odd habit, but we all have them." He shrugged.

"Let's go back to the villa," said Ruby. "We ought to show this knife to the doctor to determine if it matches the wound."

On their march homeward, they caught up with Adriana and Silvio supporting Irene as she limped along.

"How serious is her injury?" asked Ruby.

"Difficult to say," replied Silvio, "But it appears she twisted her ankle. Certainly no broken bones. If she rests it today, she ought to walk on it tomorrow."

Idris leant over to Fina. "Why is our partner lying?"

"What do you mean?"

"I'm positive Irene twisted her left ankle, but notice how she's favouring her right ankle now."

23

A trickle of hazelnut gelato ran down Fina's chin.

She wiped her face with a napkin and shovelled another large spoonful of the cool, sweet, sticky concoction into her mouth. Ruby smiled at her as she did the same with her lemon gelato. Life was becoming better.

Fabrizio had surprised them yet again with his delightful homemade recipes. The man was a wonder. What other surprises did he have in the cellar? She shivered. Better not to consider those possibilities. Enjoy the moment, she told herself, despite everything else.

Silvio had disappeared, presumably to help Irene get comfortable. They had given him the knife to examine as well. Fina was glad to hand that burden to someone else, even though she knew he could be the murderer.

Zenash and Idris had joined them for the gelato party. They too appeared considerably more relaxed with their bowls full of pistachio and chocolate flavour.

Ruby recounted their adventures to Zenash – minus Ruggero's behaviour when they found the knife.

"I cannot understand it," Zenash said. "As I told Ruby, I went to bed late and awoke late. And then you two know the rest of my morning," she said, motioning to Ruby and Fina. She held a folder aloft in triumph. "But while you were all lounging on the beach," she said with a teasing smile, "I was working."

Ruby opened the folder Zenash had handed to her. It was bursting with newspaper clippings.

"Then I remembered!" she said, holding her finger up in the air. "I had all these clippings with me. Didn't I mention I'm a terrible gossip hound?"

Idris' eyes widened. "Oh yes, so you did. But you, Zenash? Aren't you a high literary writer? You have an interest in the gutter press and celebrity gossip?"

Her laugh burbled up gradually and released itself like a delicate butterfly. "I'm full of surprises, Idris. I'm not interested in it for the reason most people are – though if I am honest with myself, I find it fascinating sometimes. Voyeurism, I suppose. Like watching a train wreck," she said, pausing. "No, I use it as fodder for the writing imagination."

Ruby slid the clippings around on the table as if they were a jigsaw. Tapping her finger against one, she asked Fina to trans-late. Fina moved closer and read aloud: "Vito Visconti worth millions. Leather magnate's profits soar." Then she selected an L-shaped clipping. "Visconti meets with Mussolini."

Ruby's eyebrows rose.

Idris made a delicate spitting noise at the name of Mussolini. Zenash nodded approval. "Go on, Fina," she said.

"Shoemaker's Spat," Fina continued. She lifted the paper as if it might crumble and began to read. "Renzo Carnevali, the famous shoe designer, has called Vito Visconti a traitor to Italy. Visconti has retaliated by demanding the government investi-gate Carnevali's business practices." Fina's eyes darted back and forth as she skimmed the clipping. She looked up. "The rest of it is the same, though it says Nicola Scarpa defended Carnevali."

Ruby handed Fina another clipping. Fina handed the clipping to Zenash. "Would you mind, Zenash? My Italian skills are limited."

Zenash took the clipping and began to read. "Carlotta Visconti seen boating with Renzo Carnevali." She put down the paper. "Nothing much more there."

"So this means Renzo has a grudge against Visconti," said Idris.

"But why would he kill Carlotta? He seems genuinely distraught over her death," said Fina.

"Perhaps he's playing a part? Perhaps he sought revenge against Visconti by killing her?" Idris speculated.

Ruby shook her head. "But Carlotta was estranged from her husband, so it wouldn't cause him much emotional harm."

"Wouldn't cause who harm?" said a voice behind Fina.

Despite his short stature, Renzo loomed behind them. "Continue, everyone. Please don't let me interrupt you," he said, as his eyes fixed on the clippings on the table.

Zenash folded her hands in her lap. "We were discussing motives. Apparently, there was no love lost between you and Vito Visconti."

Renzo's lion's mane shook itself in protest. "I despised what the man stood for, but if you believe I'd kill Carlotta for revenge, you're mistaken. I loved Carlotta ..." he trailed off. His eyes were glassy from fatigue or tears, or maybe a bit of both.

He moved toward Ruby. "I'd like to talk to you and Fina in my study, please."

She twisted round in her chair. "Without our sleuthing partners? Surely not."

He chuckled. "Yes, without your sleuthing partners."

Ruby and Fina both looked to Idris and Zenash. They nodded their assent. "I'm sure you'll tell us all the salacious details," smiled Zenash. Then she stared at Renzo innocently. "For my new book, of course, Renzo."

After wiping their sticky fingers once more on nearby napkins, they departed to the study. Renzo glanced at them over his shoulder. His eyes held unexpected fear and wariness.

A not unpleasant smell of decaying paper and tobacco smoke met their noses as they entered the study. Spying the same stack of files she had seen the previous night, Fina sat as close to them as possible. Maybe they had been shuffled so she could see new name labels.

Renzo took his place behind the desk and moved his hands into a praying position in front of his lips. Was he praying, ruminating or waiting for them to speak? She glanced over at Ruby, who sat with her hands draped over the arms of the chair.

Renzo closed his eyes. Perhaps this was a tactic to make them nervous. If so, it was certainly working.

His eyelids jerked upwards like a window shade. Touching the stack of folders, he said, "As I mentioned in my letter to Ruby, we have plenty of common interests to discuss. Carlotta's death makes this more urgent. I am afraid the authorities will most likely use this as the perfect excuse to lock me up."

"You mean because you're an anti-fascist?" asked Ruby.

"Precisely. Mussolini's government has already tried to arrest me for irregularities in my accounting practices. Fortunately, I have an excellent accountant – Miss Papas, of course – so they could not succeed," he said waving his hands at another stack of files. "But they have acted like *come le mosche al miele*. That translates as 'like flies to honey.' They're waiting. And waiting."

"Is that why you live in Sardinia? I'm aware there's a resistance movement based here – and it's physically removed from the rest of Italy," said Ruby, biting her lip.

Renzo's chair scraped against the floor with an agonising screech as he rose and began to pace in tiny circles in front of the desk. It reminded Fina of one of her dons preparing to give their favourite lecture at Oxford.

"As you say, Sardinia is removed, and there is a strong resistance movement here. As you probably guessed, Nicola is an important part of that, but mostly because he believes Sardinia ought to be independent from Italy. I cannot say I disagree with that," he said, leaning over to remove a cigarette from a box on the desk. He lit it, inhaled, and blew smoke toward the ceiling. His shoulders relaxed, and he turned and stared at Ruby. A searching stare – the kind that causes a person's eyes to dart to and fro.

"I've asked you here because we have a plan."

"I suspect I know what that might be," said Ruby. One side of her mouth curled up in a rather devious smile. "But before we proceed any further, tell me why you have a memo about Ian Clavering. Do not ask how I found out about it."

Renzo sat down and leant back in his swivel chair, rocking gently. He massaged his left temple. "Excellent. *Bene*. Well, I suppose you've passed another test, which is trying to find out everything you can about me," he smiled, taking another drag on his cigarette. "As I said, I asked you here to be a part of a plan. I have to trust you, so I had to investigate. Ian's dossier was, shall we say, procured, from the British government. He is of interest only because he's your associate."

He stubbed out his cigarette in an ashtray more thoroughly than was necessary, and glanced up at Ruby.

She nodded. "Very well. You plan to overthrow the head of the government."

Fina gasped.

Renzo turned on Fina with a ferocity she had not yet seen from their host. Then he looked at Ruby and pointed at Fina with his cigarette. "Can she be trusted?"

Ruby smiled. "Naturally. Fina has been tested many times."

A rush of shame, embarrassment and outrage flooded Fina's body. She began to rise from her seat but thought better of it. "I may have a colonial mindset – in fact, I'm certain I do – but I have no doubts about the cause, as it were. And beyond my family, Ruby is one of the few people in this world I not only trust entirely but will support in whatever she does."

Renzo threw back his head and laughed. He sat back down as if he needed to rest after the exertion from such laughing. Fina felt partially relieved, but also somewhat peeved by a man laughing at her as if she were a surprisingly adorable animal.

Holding his handkerchief to his face to wipe his eyes, the removal of it also wiped the smile from his face. "I cannot comment of what you said, Ruby, but I can say we are active in supporting the resistance. That's why I've invited everyone here this weekend. To discuss it with them individually," he sighed, leaning back in his chair. "Originally, I had planned to keep it a relative secret from each of you. But circumstances have changed," he said, rubbing his brow with evident vexation.

Fina sprung forward in her chair. "Is that why there is a printing press in the nuraghi? It must be why Idris tried to ... divert me," she trailed off, remembering that kiss. She shrank back as it dawned on her he must have kissed her just to keep her from asking more questions. Curse him.

"But how? But how did you know about that?" stammered Renzo uncharacteristically.

"He wanted to show me the nuraghi – that first night," said Fina.

"Did he now?" said Renzo, a sly smile creeping on his face. As soon as it had appeared, it vanished. "I cannot understand how he knew it was there, but I expect he surmised it was for printing leaflets."

"But to return to the changed circumstances," continued

Ruby, steering the conversation back on track. "Did Carlotta's death have something to do with your plans?"

Renzo leapt up again and began to pace with his hands in his pockets. He shrugged. "It's possible, but what's the motive? Carlotta secretly used her husband's funds to support the cause. So as far as I can tell, he is the only one who had a motive to kill her."

"So who killed Carlotta?" asked Ruby. Fina shot her a sidelong glance. Bluntness was her forte!

Renzo came to an abrupt halt, as if he had hit an invisible wall. "That's what's so maddening. I loved Carlotta. I cannot imagine who would want to do her harm. And now," he said, shrugging, and thrusting his hands deeper in his pockets, "the police will arrive and most likely detain us all under suspicion of murder. It would give them a convenient excuse to round up the resistance." Though he ran his hand through his mane decisively, it quivered nonetheless.

"Could that be the motive in and of itself?" asked Ruby. "Perhaps you have a traitor in your midst, Renzo."

24

Tap tap.

"Yes, come in," said Renzo in an exasperated voice.

Silvio entered. It would be more accurate to say Silvio's hair entered, followed by Silvio himself. Like Renzo's hand, it quivered. Though this time it might be from excitement. In the background, Fina noticed Ruggero looming like a lackey, unsure if he ought to enter or stay in the corridor.

"I'm terribly sorry to interrupt, I wanted to notify everyone as soon as possible."

"It's about the knife, isn't it?" asked Renzo.

"Yes. I confirmed the knife found in the studio was most likely the knife which killed Carlotta," he said. And then in a rather theatrical gesture, he produced the knife from behind his back, nestled in a white handkerchief. "Do any of you recognise it?"

Renzo's eyes widened. "It resembles one of the flick knife stilettos that Ruggero and Fabrizio use. They're all-purpose knives you can slip in your pocket. Ruggero uses them for fishing. If Fabrizio or Ruggero aren't carrying them around, they keep them in the kitchen."

"Who would have known about them?" asked Ruby. She took the stiletto with her handkerchief and examined it. Then she set it down on the desk, removed a piece of paper from her notebook and drew an outline of the stiletto on the paper.

Renzo appeared disconcerted by this action but did not say anything about it. "Well, that would be everyone familiar with the house," he said, shifting in his chair. His eyes darted from side to side.

"Although it could also be an outsider," said Fina. "It would be a normal feature of any household."

"Yes, but why a stiletto? It's not a useful tool, other than for letter opening. Wouldn't you take one of the many kitchen knives?" asked Ruby.

Renzo rubbed his chin. "Yes, I understand your point," he said, wincing at his own pun. "But a stiletto is easy to conceal in a pocket – and because it's a flick knife, you don't have to worry about hurting yourself."

"Do you have a stiletto as a letter opener?" asked Ruby.

Renzo waved a dismissive hand. "Yes, but how is this relevant?" he queried, pointing to the knife Silvio had brought into the study, "That's what killed her."

"Still, Renzo, would you check yours is where it's supposed to be?" said Ruby calmly.

"If you're wondering, I am the only one who has had access to it," he said, removing a necklace from under his shirt to reveal a key. "I keep this with me at all times. It unlocks the drawer containing the letter opener and a few other items of importance. I suppose someone could take it from me if I were sleeping, but that seems risky."

He moved his chair to one side and inserted the key in the lock of the top desk drawer. It slid open. He peered at the front of the drawer. "The drawer was locked. The lock hasn't been tampered with at all. And the stiletto is where it's supposed to be," he said, relocking the drawer.

"So the knife tells us little," said Fina. "Since everyone had access to it."

"Yes, and I already asked Ruggero and Fabrizio about it. They confirmed it was one of their stilettos, though neither can remember where they last saw it," said Silvio. He looked at Renzo. "Sorry, Renzo. Had to confirm your story and all that."

Renzo responded with an absentminded nod.

Ruby glanced at Fina and gave her a small nod. "Our best course of action is to continue our sleuthing, Renzo. Please let us know if you have any thoughts about what we discussed."

Ruby and Fina toddled after Silvio and Ruggero into the corridor. It was preternaturally quiet. The only sound was Ruggero cracking his knuckles at two-minute intervals. Fina winced every time he practised this habit.

Fina hissed, "What's your theory, Ruggero and Silvio? What have your investigations turned up?" It was worth a try. A direct inquiry was as good as any.

Silvio ran a finger around his collar. It looked as if someone had used extra starch to launder it. Why didn't the man opt for more comfortable clothing? Surely after a murder one was more likely to give up the usually social niceties and pretences of a weekend party.

His voice cracked. "We haven't found out much of anything, except about the knife," he said. Ruggero nudged him. "And, well, that someone is having an affair."

"Do tell," said Ruby, in her best star-struck I-love-gossip manner.

Silvio winced. Ruggero nudged him again and cracked his knuckles. Was this a warning to Silvio?

"Gina and Renzo."

"You cannot be serious," exclaimed Fina, in an outraged whisper. "Renzo was in love with Carlotta."

"It's difficult for us to believe as well," said Silvio apologetically, as if he were delivering the news of a terrible illness to a patient. "But Ruggero and I overheard them in the garden, not more than an hour ago."

"What, precisely, did they say?" asked Ruby.

Silvio ran his finger around his collar again. Ruggero stepped forward. "Gina said, 'Renzo, it's only a matter of time. Soon we'll be together. You'll see.'"

"And?" queried Ruby.

"And Renzo replied, 'But this murder changes everything,'" replied Ruggero.

"Is someone mentioning my name in vain?" came a voice from behind them. "And why are we whispering?"

Their heads turned. Nicola. He must have recently tended to his hair, as it had the requested pint of pomade to slick it all into place. He was grinning like an idiot.

"Adriana and I know who the murderer is."

25

Silence. Not even one cracked knuckle from Ruggero.

The door to the study swung open. Renzo's eyes moved from side to side. "*Oddio*! What is all this? Has anyone seen my partner, Nefeli? She was supposed to meet me a few minutes ago."

"I know why she didn't keep her appointment," said Nicola in triumph. "She's the murderer."

"Don't be daft, man, as the English say," said Renzo. "She's an accountant, not a murderer," he said, moving his head to peer behind everyone else. "And where's your partner – my sister?"

"Adriana has gone to tell the others about Nefeli."

"What makes you believe she's the murderer?" asked Ruby.

"Because she's disappeared," said Nicola. "We've searched the villa, top to bottom, as well as the island. Nowhere to be found."

"When did you last see her, Renzo?" asked Fina.

He puffed out his cheeks and then exhaled. "Must have been about an hour ago. We sat on the terrace discussing the case."

"And she didn't seem to be behaving erratically?" asked Silvio.

"Well, no. No more than usual. Nefeli was a little, well,

awkward, at the best of times. But no, she wasn't behaving out of character. Frankly, she seemed pleased with herself."

"About what?" asked Ruby.

He shook his head. "I couldn't say. She had been working on the accounts the previous evening. She said everything was splendid and it was all running smoothly. When we discussed the case, she seemed somewhat distracted," he paused, as if realising this for the first time. "But I suppose that was because of the shock. I didn't think much of it since my own head was filled with cobwebs this morning. Especially after our late night and then ... Carlotta."

Renzo held up a finger. "Wait. I expect you two didn't search the shoe room, did you?" By this time, a crowd had gathered outside the study. Using the skills she had learned from Ruby, she counted heads rapidly. All the guests, as well as Fabrizio, were assembled. Varying degrees of puzzlement, concern and shock flickered like lightning across their countenances.

Adriana stepped forward, almost like a ghost in her flowing dress. "It's the only place we did not search. That is because only you have the key, Renzo, so we thought it unlikely she would be there."

"Shoe room?" asked Nicola, now more out of professional rather than investigatory interest.

Renzo nodded and opened his desk drawer. He shuffled through papers with a look of growing panic.

"The key. It's vanished. What have you done with it, Adriana?"

"Nothing, darling. I know better than to interfere with your shoe collection."

Without another word, Renzo rushed through the crowd, miraculously avoiding shoving anyone while on his mission. He dashed down the corridor with increasing speed, then halted abruptly in front of a door that resembled a cupboard door. He shook the handle. Then he yelled, "Nefeli! Nefeli are you there?"

An efficient footstep approached, and the door swung open. Nefeli.

Fina had never heard a collective sigh of relief like that before. It sounded just like the puff of air from a fireplace bellows.

Renzo's eyes widened in anger. Nefeli took a step back into the room. He followed. At least they would be able to visit this legendary shoe collection.

"What the devil are you doing in my room?" he demanded, moving toward her like a panther.

Nefeli dropped her notebook on the floor. Graphic paper, filled with tiny handwritten numbers, spilt to the floor. "I was so upset by everything I went where no one – most especially the murderer – could find me. My nerves were shot to pieces, so I thought ... accounting soothes me, so I hoped to focus in here ... I'm so sorry if I caused anyone distress."

Renzo's shoulders slumped. "I see," he said, throwing his hands up in resignation. "I cannot say I blame you, though I thought you would notify me, your partner, at the very least. And I do not appreciate you taking the key without my permission."

Nefeli stared at her feet and was silent.

Now that they had averted a second crisis, Fina marvelled at the contents of the room. Ruby's eyes were scanning the shelves, too, smiling with delight at the shoe collection. Floor-to-ceiling bookcases displayed T-strap heels, sensible brogues, salacious open-toe evening shoes, spectator heels and sandals ranging from flat to sky-high. And the colours! Silver, scarlet, gold, rich purple, emerald green and lush azure provided a sumptuous feast for the eyes.

Renzo petted one of the closest shoes as if it were a small, furry pet. "My pride and joy. A collection of sixteenth- through nineteenth-century shoes. Please do look around now you're here." He went over to Ruby and began to tell her the history of a scandalous heel.

Nefeli grabbed Fina's arm and piloted her into the corner. "If you tell Renzo about me being in his study that first night, I'll, I'll ..." she trailed off. Her verbal communication skills exhausted, she held up a fist toward Fina's chest, well out of sight of the others.

"Understood," hissed Fina, glancing over her shoulder at Renzo and Ruby. They were engrossed by a T-strap heel in silver.

"This is all well and good," barked a voice from behind her.

"But we still have a murderer on the loose," said Irene, standing with her hands on her hips.

26

"I'm peckish," said Idris, not precisely in response to Irene's declaration. It was meant, clearly, as an additional thought. But Irene wasn't having it.

"How can you speak of food at a time like this?" she demanded. While Fina agreed it was not, perhaps, the most opportune moment for the comment, she was famished. She leant over to Ruby and whispered, "Why is Irene so agitated?"

Ruby pulled her eyes away from a gold and silver two-toned T-strap to consider Irene. She still stood, hands on hips, eyes locked on Idris, waiting for an explanation. Idris appeared unfazed by this attempt at intimidation.

Gina stepped forward to play peacemaker, a move that was a surprise to Fina. "We're all fatigued from today, and I, for one, would definitely enjoy a glass of wine."

Faces melted into smiles at the mention of the word "wine".

Building on her momentum gained from the crowd, she continued. "Fabrizio and Ruggero, how long will it take to prepare dinner?"

Fabrizio stepped forward and mumbled something in what

Fina first thought was Italian but must have been Sardinian, as she couldn't understand it. Ruggero stepped forward, or rather, lurched forward to translate. "Fabrizio has already prepared. Many are cold dishes. We can serve them soon."

"Just like revenge," said Irene. Adriana turned and stared at her friend.

Zenash put a calming hand on Irene as if she were a small child. She stepped forward. "I'm ravenous. Let's all help prepare for dinner on the terrace." She motioned to Ruggero and Fabrizio. Zenash, Ruby, Idris, Irene, Nicola and Fina – all still in pairs – followed Fabrizio to the kitchen. The others followed Ruggero, presumably to the terrace.

The kitchen was much smaller than Fina had imagined, but every inch had been used optimally. Gleaming copper pots on hooks lined the wall. Fina couldn't help but smile at the spices arranged in perfect alphabetical order on a shelf near her. The centre of the room held a large butcher's countertop, filled with trays of meat, cheese, and cold vegetables. Fabrizio waved at the dishes and then at the guests. Ruby scooped up a platter of cold asparagus in one hand and another of marinated mushrooms in the other.

A flash of black and white dashed across Fina's line of vision. A small stool sat near the butcher's block. The devious Divo had used this positioning to maximum advantage and had leapt up and snatched a large piece of prosciutto from the corner. Divo had disappeared, leaving Diva to endure the wrath of Fabrizio. "*Passa via!*" he yelled at Diva, snapping a towel at her.

Fina's grumbling stomach was jealous of Divo's risk-taking for a slice of prosciutto. She reminded herself that hunger was the best seasoning. Though she decided other seasonings worked nicely, thank you very much.

As soon as everyone had a tray or two, they made a procession line out of the kitchen. Ruby bumped Fina and gave her a glance which said she should remain behind. Fina adjusted her trays in an elaborate fashion so as to let Fabrizio be the last one to leave, though he peered at Fina suspiciously. As if she might follow the cat's lead and snatch a whole tray of prosciutto for herself.

Ruby popped around the doorway and said, "All clear. Here," she said, pulling out a slip of paper from her dress pocket. "Gina dropped it in the corridor when we all left the shoe room. Can you translate it?"

Though Ruby had smoothed the paper and folded it like a proper letter, it looked as if it had been crumpled into a ball. Fina set down her tray of olives – not before popping two in her mouth – and sat down on a nearby stool. She needed brain food.

She read aloud:

GINA,

We must speak. It is more urgent than ever.
Silvio.

FINA SMILED as Ruby munched on a spear of asparagus. "A love letter? But that's odd since Silvio told us she was having an affair with Renzo. My goodness, these people lead lives as complicated as a hank of yarn."

Ruby grabbed her tray and walked toward the door. "But couldn't it also be about something else – non-romantic, I mean – that he needs to tell her?"

"Related to the murder?"

"Perhaps. The other difficulty is that we haven't any idea when Silvio wrote this note."

"Let's try to sit next to them at dinner. We can continue our sleuthing."

"Agreed. We need to find this murderer. And fast."

"Why fast?"

"Because I have a bad feeling, Feens. The next murder is coming. According to my grandmother, what goes badly in the morning cannot become good in the evening."

Fina stopped in the doorway. She wasn't sure why, but she had a premonition. "Let's set these trays down back in the kitchen. Something fishy is going on."

"Too right, Feens. This fishiness reeks to high heaven. But what are you thinking?" she said, moving back into the kitchen.

"Let's go to our rooms."

"Lead on, intuitive one."

They reached the top of the back staircase. The corridor was quiet. Fina waved Ruby down the corridor to their rooms.

Ruby held a restraining hand on Fina's arm. She pointed to Carlotta's room with the theatre painting adorning the door.

"How appropriate," whispered Fina wryly.

Carlotta's door was unlocked and made mercifully little noise as they padded over the large rugs covering the entire floor. The room was spacious – perhaps twice the size of their own – with a gigantic four-poster bed pushed up against one wall. It was neat and tidy, most likely because Carlotta had just arrived. Fina surmised she was normally not the tidiest person by what appeared to be a small explosion of make-up and toiletries on the dressing table.

Ruby stepped toward the bed. Fina's eyes widened in horror. A lump underneath the covers suspiciously resembled Carlotta. She supposed they had to put her somewhere. Better than outside. She shuddered.

Glancing back at Fina, Ruby whispered, "Why don't you have a poke around while I have a look at Carlotta? It will be better if you're distracted."

Fina nodded gratefully and walked to the other side of the room. She stuck her head into the wardrobe, and after a few minutes of poking around, emerged again. She peered at the items on the dressing table. At least ten lipstick tubes littered the surface, matched only by an army of bottles of various creams and tonics. She opened the sponge bag set off to the side.

She removed the contents one by one. Beyond the expected toiletries, she found a red and yellow tin of capsules which read *Ergoapiol*. The description on the front indicated it relieved "menstrual disorders" and was only to be prescribed under a physician's guidance. That would be a blessed relief if it worked.

Fina spun round to find Ruby sitting on a chair, scribbling in her notebook.

"Find anything of interest, Feens?" she asked, barely looking up from her task.

"No, not anything of real interest," she said, pausing. "Have you ever used these before? Are they effective?"

Ruby took the tin from Fina and studied it. "I've heard of this before. But I cannot remember where and when. Let me make a note."

"Could take a few? I'll need them soon. And you know how unbearable I can be!"

Ruby smiled. "You and me both ... I wouldn't take them, if I were you. It says under physician's guidance. But you might ask the other women guests – if you feel comfortable with them."

Fina nodded sadly and replaced the items in the sponge bag.

"What did you ... find?" she asked. "Do you mind if we go into the corridor? I cannot stand to be in here any longer."

As they moved into the hallway, Ruby recounted her findings. "First, I noticed, to put it politely, there weren't the usual signs of drowning – her lungs were their normal shape. There are cases of drowning where the lungs were not misshapen, but most of the time they are."

"Selkies and kelpies, Miss Ruby Dove. What have you been reading in your spare time?"

"Well, I've combined my interests in chemistry and now in sleuthing. So I have to admit I've been reading a bit on pathology."

"Better you than me," said Fina. "What else did you find out, Dr Dove?"

She smiled. "Well, I could be wrong, but I don't believe that knife was the knife that killed Carlotta – or the one which was used to stab her. I took the drawing and measured the entry wound. The knife we found in the studio is much too large to make an incision that deep."

"So Silvio is lying?"

Ruby tapped her teeth with her pencil. "Maybe, though maybe he just wanted to avoid the gruesome task. After all, what does it matter if she were drowned? And that knife was accessible to everyone, so it doesn't tell us much."

"Do you think he did it?"

Ruby shook her head. "Seems unlikely, not only because he's missing a motive, but because the false identification would draw attention to himself. He might be protecting someone, though. Maybe he knows something. We ought to confront him."

Fina crossed her arms and stared at Ruby. "That's not a good idea. If he is the murderer, then he'll definitely come after us! If he's not the murderer, he may still put us in danger if he's protecting someone."

"I hadn't considered that, but I think you might be right."

"Look!" hissed Fina.

The door to Fina's room stood open a half inch.

Ruby and Fina took positions on either side of the door. Ruby held up one a one finger signal and pushed the door open.

"Idris!" cried Fina.

Idris dropped Fina's notebook to the floor. He stood there, mouth gaping open in what was surely his only unattractive pose.

Her knees began to wobble. First the diversion away from the printing press, now this. He must be the traitor.

"Double selkies and kelpies. You'd better explain yourself and quickly," said Fina with her hands on her hips.

Ruby said nothing, but her jaw muscles were working as rapidly as a squirrel chewing the first nuts of the season after a long winter.

"I thought ... Renzo said," said Idris. He threw up his hands. "It doesn't matter now. I decided you two were traitors, or spies supporting the fascists."

Ruby and Fina stared at one another.

"But that's what I thought about you," said Fina. "First you try to distract me from the printing press and then you don't want to speak to me. Next I find you searching my room."

"Fina is right. This appears rather suspicious, Idris," said Ruby, mirroring Fina's hands-on-hips gesture. The two of them formed a formidable block to the doorway.

"If you don't support the fascists, why does Fina's notebook have so many newspaper clippings about Italian politics?"

The nerve of the man. Fina rose to and snagged the bait. Quite deliberately. "I'm a student of political history. That's why.

Now are you going to explain yourself or ought we start a conversation with everyone at dinner about you?"

Fina swore Idris' body shrank in size. He shrugged. "There's nothing to explain. I apologise most wholeheartedly to both of you, but particularly to Fina," he said. There was that unnerving gaze again. Fina stared at an insipid painting on the wall as if it were the Mona Lisa. "I thought you were the traitors and you thought I was the traitor. End of story."

"Why did you pretend you weren't acquainted with Zenash when we were at breakfast at the hotel in Terranova Pausania?" asked Fina.

"Breakfast..." he said, looking puzzled. "Oh, yes. Breakfast. Zenash and I have a habit of pretending we don't know one another if we're around someone we haven't met, or haven't come to trust at all. It's not that Nefeli made us particularly nervous. Old habits are difficult to break. That's all," he finished, triumphant.

Fina relaxed a little. "But why did you try to keep me from talking about the printing press?" Her eyes still fixed on the painting. She knew if she glanced at him, she would lose her resolve.

"Honestly, I was unaware it was there. But when I spotted it, I realised it must have been connected to Renzo's plans. I had just met you, and hadn't any idea of the role, if any, you played in our little drama. That's why I tried to divert you." He paused and stared at Ruby.

As if on cue, Ruby rummaged in her handbag as if she had lost her only heirloom piece of jewellery. She was entirely focused on her task.

Idris carried on, coming closer to Fina. His voice was soft. "But I assure you that had you been anyone else, I would have diverted you by simply leading you out of the darkness."

Fina involuntarily scratched her neck lightly. The room had

surely become much warmer in the last minute or so. She stood there, unable to speak.

Ruby looked up from her intense search and said, "Let's all go downstairs to dinner. They all might think we've been murdered."

28

Despite the events of the last twenty-four hours, dinner was a lively event. Fina reflected on other dinners she had attended where a murder had been committed. Unlike those events, which had often been sombre affairs, this one was filled with excited chatter. What all those dinners shared, however, was an undercurrent of nervous tension. The tension was outward rather than inward. Except Idris and Irene, who both sat quietly, as if they were eating dinner by themselves. Fina tried to focus on the other guests' conversations, and not withdraw inward to mull over Idris' behaviour.

Adriana put on her best show as a host, refilling everyone's glasses as soon as they tipped under the halfway mark. Fabrizio rushed back and forth from the kitchen, clearing away empty platters and bringing new ones piled high with food. Everyone certainly had an appetite. Fina's stomach was about to burst. As she reluctantly put her fork down, she decided she'd better concentrate on Ruby's directions to engage with Gina. Ruby was already in deep conversation with Silvio.

Small talk was never Fina's strong suit, even at the best of times. Even if she didn't succeed at it, at least the wine dulled the sting of social awkwardness.

She waved her glass in Gina's direction. Her mind raced about what little she knew of Gina. A *lettore*. A dancer. Jealous. Adulterer?

"Do you make ballet shoes?" Fina asked as her wine glass spilt a little onto the white tablecloth. Fina felt a wave of nausea as the red against white backdrop reminded her of blood.

"*Scusi*?" asked Gina who wiped her delicate hands on a napkin.

"I thought the two would go together – since you're a dancer and part of the shoemaking business."

The wrinkles of concentration on her forehead washed away. "Oh, yes. I can see how you'd believe that. I make my own shoes for dancing, but we don't produce them for anyone else."

"Why not?"

"Lately I've been getting these headaches which make it challenging for me to do much of anything. Besides, it would be too time-consuming, even if I weren't the one to direct it. Though Nicola suggested we make them into everyday shoes women could wear."

"With heels?"

Gina laughed. "No, no heels. It must seem inconceivable, but it's difficult to always walk in heels. Not so good for the posture. Me, I try to wear sandals or slippers whenever possible," she said, pointing to the silver slippers on her feet.

"I suppose they'd be convenient for a rendezvous, wouldn't they?"

Pursing her lips and then breaking into a smile, she replied, "Very convenient."

Blast it. The woman was being coy. Time for a different tack.

"I never found out how everyone knew each other. Obviously, you and Nicola know Renzo, but were you acquainted with any of the others, such as Silvio or Adriana?"

"We knew Adriana through Renzo. And we had visited the island once before, so I met Ruggero and Fabrizio. None of the others, though."

"And Silvio?"

She squinted up at the sky. "Silvio. Well, yes, of course. Through Renzo. He has been helpful in answering medical questions for us both."

Fina winced as a stomach cramp shot through her abdomen on cue. She said in a conspiratorial voice, hand cupping one side of her mouth, "Speaking of doctors, are you familiar with Ergoapiol? It's supposed to help calm cramps, if you know what I mean." She rubbed her stomach.

Gina immediately fell into the trap. "Oh yes. I have dreadful cramps. I asked Silvio, during a confidential appointment, if he had anything he could give me, and he gave me those pills. I'm taking them now," she said with a giggle. "And I feel just spiffing – for the moment," she said, taking a healthy swig of her wine as if to make the point.

"So your relationship with Silvio is purely professional?" The moment Fina uttered these words, she knew she had made a blunder.

Gina's eyes narrowed. "Yes, of course it's *professional*. What other kind of relationship would I have with him?" She threw down her napkin. "Please excuse me."

Fina was saved from further unproductive conversation with Gina by Idris' inquiry about dancing. The dinner had transitioned into the nibbling phase – when everyone has finished but still picks at the detritus on the table as they carry on drinking wine. Fabrizio and Ruggero had disappeared, presumably to attend to something in the kitchen. Zenash had left to retrieve cigarettes, and Adriana said she wanted to walk a few steps over to an outcrop to contemplate the sunset. Irene had been absent for ages.

Ruby sat next to Silvio, chatting away. She rubbed her nose at least three times, a sure sign she was fibbing. Though she smiled at Silvio and appeared relaxed, Fina sensed that not all was well, especially when her eyes slid toward Fina in a worried way.

Out of the corner of her eye, she sensed a figure approaching. Fina had almost a sixth sense when it came to observing body language, especially when it wasn't in her direct line of vision. This figure was all wrong.

Renzo leapt out of his seat.

"You must be Mr Hayford! *Benvenuto!*" cried Renzo, first sticking out his hand and then dropping it in favour of an embrace.

"Please, call me Pixley," said Pixley Hayford, giving a little bow to everyone around him.

Fina felt her chair moving backwards, as if of its own accord. Somehow, she ended up sitting on the stone terrace.

"Fina!" cried Gina, as she bent over to help her up.

Selkies and kelpies. She got to her feet and brushed herself off. Moving as nonchalantly as she could, she joined the growing group around the new guest.

As Pixley was now encircled with curious guests, Fina whispered to Ruby, "Did you realise he would be joining us? And why? I have so many questions, Ruby Dove!"

Ruby put a hand on Fina. "I know, I know, I ought to have told you."

"You mean you knew?!" cried Fina, then lowering her voice as Gina peered over her shoulder in a perplexed manner.

"Yes, well. A little," Ruby said, smoothing her hair. "I received a letter from Wendell when we were in Terranova Pausania. He swore me to secrecy – he said I couldn't tell even you. Wendell was worried about us. He knew better than to imply that we couldn't take care of ourselves, but he was concerned that James would follow us. Because Wendell had to return to duty on a ship, he asked Pixley to join us. I arranged it with Renzo, who agreed once he vetted Pixley's credentials as a sympathetic journalist."

"But why Pixley? He's not precisely, well, the first person I'd turn to in an international game of espionage," she said, looking at the bespectacled, squat man grinning at the guests. Bald as an egg. He was muscular, though. Fina felt ashamed, so she amended her statement. "Not that I think we fit the idea of a spy, either. And I am happy to see him. He's great fun," she said.

"I know what you mean, Feens," replied Ruby. "Pixley is useful because he's a journalist. James wouldn't dare to do much of anything even if he figured out a way onto the island. Unfortunately, Pixley was held up from joining us in Terranova Pausania."

"How did Wendell convince Pixley to travel all this way?"

"He provided the kind of bait you'd offer any journalist – the possibility of a juicy story," she paused. "At the very least, he could write a story about Italian politics and the colonisation of Ethiopia."

"Well, it is a delightful surprise. And a relief given all that has happened. Maybe he can help us unravel this particular mystery."

Finally, the crowd parted as several guests left and returned to the table. Fina rushed up to Pixley. She threw her arms around him and gave him a great squeeze. As she hugged Pixley, a look of surprise spread rapidly on Idris' face. Good. Serves him right. Besides, she wasn't satisfied with his explanation of his room-searching activities.

"My, you are on rather friendly terms," said Adriana drily.

Pixley grinned at Adriana and offered her his hand. "Pixley

Hayford. I'm awfully sorry to gatecrash your dinner party like this, but my ferry from the mainland was cancelled. I paid a local fisherman to take me here in their boat."

"Renzo invited you?" asked Adriana incredulously. Renzo loomed up behind her.

"Yes, I invited him to our little party. I knew Ruby and Fina were friends with him."

As if he anticipated the next question, Pixley interjected, "I'm a journalist."

Adriana's neck craned to stare at Renzo.

Pixley wiped his bald head. "I'm a journalist who's decidedly on the anti-fascist, or should I say, anti-colonial side. No need to worry. I can be discreet."

"Are you from St. Kitts, just like Ruby?" asked Adriana.

"No, no. Born and bred in London. My family came to London from Ghana in the seventeenth century."

Renzo physically intervened between Adriana and Pixley. "This calls for a celebration!" he declared.

"Wait," said Idris. "You must have come by boat. Did the fisherman moor his boat on the dock? We all need to get to shore. And fast."

Pixley peered at him quizzically. "He let me off at the dock a few minutes ago."

A collective groan ensued.

"Why is it so urgent to get to the mainland?" asked Pixley.

Renzo intervened. "I'll let everyone else tell you about it while I find those special bottles of wine for you in the cellar."

29

Fina shivered, and it wasn't because of the waning temperature. Her ability to sense atmosphere told her something was wrong. Very wrong. Despite the appearance of an amiable new dinner guest, her other dining companions embodied an awkward tension.

Idris creaked in his chair as he shifted, crossing and uncrossing his legs. Nefeli fidgeted with her watch. Adriana rearranged the folds of her clothes. Zenash puffed languidly on a cigarette. Ruby smoothed her hair. Pixley swung one of his legs like a child sitting on a chair which is too tall for them. Ruggero cracked his knuckles. Fabrizio was absent. So was Irene.

Slap. Slap.

Footsteps, swift footsteps, now running, came around the terrace. Renzo's mane was sticking up every which way. And his shoes were untied.

"Come, come! You must all come!" he exclaimed, turning around, and dashing back the way he had come.

Fina heard but didn't see seats turning over in the rush to follow Renzo. Ruggero took the lead, striding, as his long legs carried him just as briskly as those who were of shorter stature but running.

She couldn't spot Renzo, but she followed Ruggero's head. It disappeared as he went into the cellar. Ruby squeezed Fina's hand reassuringly as they all made their way, single file, down into the cellar.

Zenash screamed. Then Idris. Then Adriana yelled "*Oddio!*"

The sweet smell of fermenting grapes wafted up from the vat. She peered over the edge just as Zenash grasped her shoulders to pull her away. All she spied was a toe. A purple toe. Irene.

Suddenly the sweet smell turned her stomach. A gush of acid forced its way upward through her throat. She plopped down on a nearby step where Ruby was also sitting. She had her head between her legs. Seeing Ruby like that forced the nausea away. She put a hand on Ruby's back and said, "Breathe, Ruby, breathe."

While she was rubbing Ruby's back she stared absently around the room. Bottles lined the walls. Canvas covered what was presumably winemaking equipment in a corner of the room. A small bookcase was lined with a mishmash of decaying books. Nothing appeared out of place or any different than what they had seen the day before.

Renzo ordered them all to leave, save Silvio and Ruggero. Guests trudged up the winding stairs to the drawing room, where they flopped down on sofas and chairs in front of the large windows overlooking the sea.

"We would like your attention," said Renzo, ascending the staircase with an exaggerated gait.

Silvio's hair emerged from behind him, followed by Silvio. Ruggero was next. Fina winced as she watched him bump his head on the entrance to the staircase. He held a brown cloth in his hand. It resembled a tea towel. Rubbing his head with one hand, he offered Silvio the cloth with another.

Silvio cleared his throat several times. He held the cloth aloft as if he were about to auction a priceless painting. "As I'm sure you all suspected, Irene is dead."

Adriana, who had been standing near the window, collapsed into a nearby chair. Nefeli leant over and stroked her arm as if she were a cat. Soft sobs came from the corner. The softness touched Fina and the tears soon welled up in her eyes as well.

"We found this cloth stuffed in her mouth," continued Silvio. He waved his hand slowly around the room.

"Does anyone recognise it?" asked Renzo.

Everyone shook their heads or stared out the window.

Ruby stood up. "May I take a closer look?"

Renzo proffered her the handkerchief. She marched over to the window and held it up to the light. Spinning on her heel, she said to Fabrizio, "May I use a few items in your kitchen? I'd like to try an experiment with the handkerchief."

Renzo nodded his approval to Fabrizio. As she passed Fina, Ruby whispered, "I'll return soon. Take notes while I'm gone."

"Well, what do we do now?" asked Zenash. "All sit here all night? If we're going to do that, I'll need espresso. Otherwise, I propose we all go to bed and lock our doors."

Idris shook his head. "We should all stay here. It's safer that way."

"And sleep upright in the chairs?" asked Gina incredulously.

"Better than finding yourself dead," he retorted.

"Dear ones, no need to quarrel," Renzo said, turning to Pixley. "Although it is an imposition, I realise, would you escort each guest to their rooms? You are the only one not involved in these murders, so everyone ought to feel safe with you."

"Of course, though it will be a slow process," replied Pixley. "I can take small groups at a time." He began with Zenash and Nefeli. Soon the room had emptied, with Renzo being almost the last to go. Fina had asked to go last. She sat, shivering underneath a blanket even though the night breeze through the windows was still warm.

"Whew. Glad I've finished with that," said Pixley, wiping his brow as he sat down on a nearby sofa.

"Are you sure they're all locked in their rooms?" asked Fina.

"Yes, although it doesn't prevent one of them from getting out and roaming the hallways," said Pixley. "It only protects them from an intruder."

"Even so, let's go outside to talk. I don't want to take a risk of someone eavesdropping from the staircase."

"How about a glass of wine?" asked Pixley.

Fina turned to glare at him. He shrugged. "Sorry. That wasn't considerate."

He smiled as he removed a flask. "I have whisky, though, and I can guarantee it isn't made from grapes."

They took turns taking a swig from his flask as they sat out on the terrace, swatting away the occasional mosquito. Fina provided Pixley as brief an explanation of the events of the past few hours as best she could.

"Now, before anything else happens, tell me everything you've learned about any of the guests. You must have some information about them," said Fina.

"Well, yes," said Pixley. "Renzo implied I ought to do as much in his invitation letter. I do know a few things about Zenash and Idris."

"Go on. Leave nothing out."

"Zenash is joyful company, but I cannot but help but feel there is an underlying sadness there. I've seen her a few times at parties in London, though we've never been introduced. I know her through friends of friends."

"And Idris?"

A light, tapping footstep approached. Ruby emerged from the drawing room, a triumphant smile plastered on her face.

"Ruby Dove! What are you doing wandering about by yourself? What happened to Fabrizio?"

"Oh, I told him I would be fine. He just shrugged and continued to slice up vegetables. I gather that cooking relieves him from strain. So I left him to it."

"Will he'll be fine down there by himself?"

"Why not? Besides, he has plenty of sharp objects at his disposal down there should someone try something foolish."

Pixley shuddered.

Ruby pulled up a chair and folded her hands in her lap. "Sorry, I have something important to tell you, but I want to hear whatever you were about to say about Idris," she said, looking at Pixley.

"He is a Berber Jew in exile from Libya. Like Zenash, he desperately wants the Italians to leave their colonial adventures behind."

"We found out that much," said Fina. "Anything else?" she said, hearing the hopeful note in her own voice.

Pixley shook his head.

"He has a penchant, shall we say, for Miss Aubrey-Havelock," said Ruby.

"Does he now?" said Pixley with a slow grin at Fina.

Fina looked away. "Rubbish!"

"Sorry, Feens," said Ruby apologetically. "I couldn't help myself." She paused. "Now, on to my news. The handkerchief was stained. That much must have been obvious – stained by the grape juice. I cleaned it up and found the original piece of fabric had been another colour."

"Selkies and kelpies – don't keep us in suspense. Tell us!" exclaimed Fina.

"It was yellow."

Pixley let out a low whistle. "You know what that means, don't you?"

Fina blinked.

Pixley twirled his spectacles. "It means someone was a traitor."

30

———

"So, Irene must have been a traitor," said Fina.

They sat in silence. The night was still, except for the occasional screeches of a nocturnal creature – bats? – and the waves lapping against the rocks.

Pixley jiggled his leg. "What kind of traitor? A traitor to the fascists or anti-fascists?"

Ruby bit her lip. "My guess is she was a traitor to anti-fascist forces, since that's why we're all here."

"You mean Irene was going to foil the plans against the ..." Fina glanced at Ruby for permission to finish her sentence.

"Yes, plans to overthrow Mussolini," said Ruby simply.

Pixley's twirling spectacles nearly launched into orbit. He caught them just in time. "You're saying you're all here to coordinate a plan to overthrow the Italian government?"

"When you say it like that, it sounds rather dramatic, doesn't it?" said Ruby.

"I should say so," responded Pixley. "It is rather dramatic. I can't take it in."

"That's why we have representatives from all of the Italian colonies here," said Fina, gratified that for once she had information in a murder case she could explain to others. "Or, I ought to say, places which are resisting Italian colonisation."

"Wait a moment," said Pixley. "What if Renzo invited everyone here under the auspices of that plan, but he actually had other motives."

"Such as what, precisely?" asked Fina.

"I agree with you, Pixley," said Ruby. "At least I think so."

"Tell me what's been rolling around in that fabulous mind of yours," said Pixley.

"Well, ever since Fina ran into those files about individual guests on Renzo's desk – coupled with the murder of Carlotta – I began to wonder if there was another, related reason for asking us all here," she said. She rose and began to pace in small circles on the terrace. If she took her accustomed large path of pacing, she would have fallen off the cliff. "Renzo has been trying to find out which one of us is a traitor to the cause."

"Or, at the very least, testing everyone before he moves forward with the plan," said Fina, warming to the subject.

"That is a plausible story," said Pixley, wiping his bald head with a handkerchief. "Let's read those files. Everyone's gone to bed."

"Pixley Hayford, you're a born sleuth," giggled Ruby, rising and moving toward the outside entrance to the study. She jiggled the French windows, but they were locked.

"Should we go around to the inside entrance?" asked Fina.

"No," whispered Ruby. "I expect it will be locked as well. Besides, there's less chance of us being caught from the outside."

Pixley held up a small screwdriver in triumph. He plunged it into the lock.

"Shhh!" hissed Ruby. "Can't you be a little quieter?"

"Sorry. This is what it takes. I'm not a professional."

After what seemed to be interminable seconds of gentle rattling, Fina heard a gratifying clunk.

The window creaked open slowly. Pixley adjusted his spectacles and gestured toward Ruby and Fina to enter first.

Fina hoisted up her skirt and stepped over the bottom frame of the French windows into the study. She heard a ripping sound behind her. Looking down, she saw a bit of fabric had torn off in the door frame. "Blast it. My gown caught on the window," she said, crouching down toward the door frame.

"Eeeeeeee ..." cried Pixley as he fell on top of Fina.

"What the devil?" hissed Fina.

Ruby helped Pixley to his feet. "It's not Pixley's fault," she said. A bat just flew very near us.

"Isn't that just a myth that they get tangled in your hair?" asked Fina.

Ruby giggled. "Well, Pixley has nothing to worry about on that score."

"My hairstyle is the height of fashion, thank you very much," said Pixley with an air of confidence.

"I'm surprised we haven't caused the entire house party to come and see who is making this racket," said Fina, as she finally removed the torn piece of fabric.

"They're probably too frightened to leave their rooms," said Ruby.

"Except for the murderer," said Pixley, shuddering. "Let's get this over with as quickly as possible." He stepped into the darkness.

Fina's small torch created a spotlight effect on the room. First it flashed every which way, as if it had a life of its own. Soon she had tamed it to focus on Ruby's hands as she sorted through the files on the desk.

She waved Fina and Pixley over closer as she opened a file to read. The words "Idris Maghur" were scrawled across the top. Fina gulped.

Idris Maghur
 Born: Tripolitania, 1908.
 Residence: London
 Profession: Architect

RELEVANT SKILLS: *International relationships with other anti-fascists. Spatial and sketching skills will be invaluable in planning.*

DESCRIPTION: *His need to avenge family will make him loyal, but it also may cause him to deviate from plans if he perceives them to be not aligned with his goals. Also apparently abhors violence. The only act which might move him to violence would be disloyalty. Prefers to work by himself than with others.*

"IF CARLOTTA or Irene were disloyal, would he kill them?" hissed Pixley.

Fina shook her head. Ruby said nothing but moved on to the next file which contained a typewritten memo with scribbles lacing the margins.

Zenash Araya Ezana
 Born: Ankober, 1895.
 Residence: London?
 Profession: Author

RELEVANT SKILLS: *International relationships with other anti-fascists. Writing skills invaluable in producing propaganda.*

DESCRIPTION: Entirely committed to the campaign and a natural leader. Great flexibility and adaptability, but concerned about possible threats to family in Ethiopia. Symbolism important.

"ODDS BODKINS! WAS IT ZENASH?" queried Pixley.

Fina froze. Slow, barely perceptible footsteps approached in the corridor. Ruby held up a hand to Pixley's mouth as he was about to open it again.

The footsteps stopped. Fina held her breath. Should they try to hide? That would only make more noise.

She breathed easier as she focused on the clock ticking from somewhere inside the study. Tick tick tick. Surely whoever it was in the corridor had gone. But then they would have heard their footsteps walking away.

The stack of files leant at a precarious angle, already beginning to slide off the desk. Her stomach twisted in knots as she watched the paper files slide to the floor. She tried to catch them but was too late. The whole process seemed to take minutes, but the result was immediate.

The footsteps came more rapidly now, toward the study.

Ruby motioned them all toward the window. Fina didn't need to be told this twice. Her natural urge was to turn and run. And run she did.

31

Fina trained her torchlight on Ruby's back, as much to light Ruby's way as to follow her to wherever she was running. As they reached the pathway away from the villa, they slowed down due to the small wooden bridge which crossed a small stream. She couldn't hear Pixley's footsteps behind her. Why wasn't he with them? She saw two figures behind them, moving toward them at a fast pace.

"Ruby! They're gaining on Pixley!" she hissed as she saw one figure gaining on another.

In a moment of indecision, they stood fixed to the spot. Fina heard a mosquito buzzing near them. And footfall, heavy footfall.

"Pixley will catch up. To the studio!" said Ruby in a whispering roar. Fina stood frozen. Everything in her mind was telling her to run, but her body remained out of loyalty and fear.

Ruby cried "You can't save him! Hurry!"

Fina's legs sprang into action. The torchlight wobbled as they dashed toward the cliff in the dark, as much from the rough terrain as from Fina's shaking hands.

A sliver of roof slipped into view from the hill, lit by

suddenly strong moonlight. Fina's racing mind had never been so happy to see a shack.

The moon continued to guide their way to the studio. Fina prayed the doors were open. Ruby rattled the doors in vain. Fina dared not glimpse behind her, though the thumping noise came closer.

"Quickly! Out of my way!" said Fina, as if another person had taken over her body. She wrapped her torch and her hand into the folds of her dress. Fist tightened, she took a deep breath and punched through one of the glass panes near the doorknob.

A satisfying tinkling of glass resulted, shards falling on the ground, sparkling from the moonlight hitting them from above. Still keeping her hand inside her dress, she looped her hand through the jagged pane, wincing as she did so. Presto! The door opened.

They pushed their way inside. Ruby slammed the doors shut and dragged the wardrobe near the door across the French windows. Just as it fit into place, blocking the smashed window pane, Fina heard footsteps outside. Then she saw a figure in a hooded cape. She froze, remembering her grandmother's folk tales about the Irish Dullahan, a headless horseman. A fairy creature who roams about, carrying his head with him. Fina cried out as she also remembered that when the Dullahan is not on his horse, a person is going to die.

Ruby shook Fina.

Dashing around the studio to find whatever heavy objects they could, Fina and Ruby moved a desk and chair in front of the opening. The door rattled, then rattled more. Again, Fina stood in horror, as she knew locked or blocked doors would never stop the Dullahan.

Then silence.

Fina squeezed Ruby's hand in the darkness. The torch had gone out, most likely broken by the window smashing. All she saw was moonlight filtering in over the top of the desk, chair and wardrobe barrier.

Ruby mouthed the words "Are they gone?"

Fina tried to shrug her shoulders but found they were frozen in place around her ears. She twisted her face in what she hoped was a message of utter confusion.

Ruby gripped her shoulder so tightly that Fina repressed the instinct to cry out in pain. Touching her ear, Ruby motioned to her to listen.

Water. Or liquid. Sloshing around. And it wasn't the sea.

"They'll burn us alive!" cried Ruby, letting go of any need to be quiet.

Fina's already tightened chest threatened to collapse in on itself. Taking in every bit of the room, she closed her eyes and remembered back to the first day they were in the studio with Irene. There had been a breeze, coming from somewhere in the studio that wasn't a door or the window. The easel. Covered in canvas in the corner. Dashing over to the easel, Fina flung off the dusty, heavy canvas. There was just enough light to spot a small panel in the back, about the size of a door for an elf. She pounded on it with her fist, and then her foot.

More sloshing.

"Hurry, Feens!" cried Ruby who had also taken to kicking in the small door.

Finally, it burst open. Fina hunched over and squeezed through the opening. On the other side, Fina tore at the opening to make it bigger for the taller Ruby.

A great whoosh. And then everything was illuminated.

"Ruby!" screamed Fina.

A cloud of smoke enveloped her as she sat on a dirt knoll behind the studio. Flames shot into the air in front of her, like demons reaching for the sky.

"Ruby!" she yelled again, coughing.

She felt herself being tugged backwards by a powerful pair of hands. "Let me go," she screeched, wriggling and fighting the hands. The more she wriggled and yelled, the more smoke she inhaled.

Then, just as suddenly as the hands had descended on her, she lapsed into a dreamlike state. Great big puffy balls of wool filled her head. Her mind raced, trying to tell her body to react, but her body would not respond.

As she drifted into unconsciousness, her mind's eye filled with flowers and farm animals.

32
———

Pain shot through Fina's neck as she jerked her head upwards.

Above her, she surveyed grey cotton clouds against a black backdrop. There it was again. That noise. That awful noise. Like a squealing pig. She jumped up but soon fell back down again as her world began to spin.

"Feens! Fina, where are you?" came Ruby's voice from somewhere below.

"I'm here, Ruby! Listen for my voice and move toward it," she yelled back.

"I can't. I'm stuck. Walk toward my voice," she replied.

Since walking was out of the question, Fina crawled toward her on her belly. She winced as her belly hit knobbly objects on the ground. Soon she was closer to the fire. She spotted the top of Ruby's head, bent to the side, resting against a hillside.

"Help me – my foot is caught underneath this root," she said, pointing toward her ankle.

"What happened?" asked Fina as she pushed and pulled at the root. Good thing she had started those tennis lessons. Her arm muscles were existent for once in her life.

"Don't talk, Feens. Save your breath – there's still a lot of smoke," whimpered Ruby.

Fina continued to work in silence. Soon Ruby's foot was free, and they both crawled as far as they could away from the studio.

They both opened their mouths like guppies gasping for air as they escaped the worst of the smoke.

"If you didn't pull me away from the fire, who did?" asked Fina.

Ruby shook her head weakly and rested it on a patch of grass.

"And who, or what, produced that squealing sound?" asked Fina, talking more to the tree branch nearest to her than to her catatonic friend.

"It was the murderer who squealed," said a voice from behind her.

"Pixley!" cried Fina.

The light from the studio fire provided just enough illumination to see their friend standing behind them, dishevelled and discombobulated. His usual dapper clothing was askew, torn, and dirty. But he had a great Cheshire cat grin on his face.

"What are you two doing out on this fine night?" he said sardonically, dropping down beside them. At least one of them hadn't lost their sense of humour.

Ruby's eyes shot open like a cat startled out of a deep sleep. "Pixley, we must get to the villa. The murderer will surely find us!"

He wiped his head in a backwards–forwards motion. "No need to worry about that. The murderer is gone."

"What do you mean, 'gone'?" asked Fina.

"As they were dousing the studio with liquid – from a large metal container – to set the studio on fire, I came up behind them and put them in a chokehold. They had already lit the match. We struggled and the match escaped to the ground.

Before I knew it, the studio was on fire, and so was the murderer. At least I assume it must have been the murderer."

"So the screaming came from the murderer, since they were on fire?" asked Fina.

"Yes," said Pixley sadly. "Poor chap. No one ought to die like that. He jumped into the sea. Must have seemed like the only plausible course of action when you're on fire."

"Why do you say 'chap'? Do you know who it was?" asked Fina.

"No, I just assumed it was a man," said Pixley. "I'm not sure why."

Ruby had closed her eyes. They weren't going to get any immediate information from her.

"Wait," said Fina, gawking at Pixley. "Were you the one who pulled me from the fire?"

He smiled and pushed back his spectacles on his nose. They were the one item which had somehow survived his ordeal.

"Wendell would never forgive me if anything happened to you two," he laughed.

Fina gave out a weak half-cough, half-laugh. Ruby rolled over onto her side to face them. "Let's just get back to the villa. I'm cold."

Pixley nodded. "I don't want to leave you two alone out here while I go to get help."

"We'll be fine," said Ruby. "No one will harm us." She rolled back onto her other side.

Soon a small band of guests arrived, carrying makeshift stretchers of large swathes of canvas. Must be from the cellar, shuddered Fina.

Though she couldn't see anything, as she was being carried

like she was in a procession, she enjoyed being suspended in the air and wrapped in the comfort of the canvas. She felt herself drifting into sleep or unconsciousness – she couldn't tell which – as the hum of voices enveloped her auditory nerves.

After Silvio and Pixley attended to the pair to make sure nothing was broken, Ruby insisted they both take baths.

"Psst ... Feens," whispered Ruby when they met in the upstairs hallway on their way to begin their baths.

"What is it?" asked Fina.

"I want you to draw your bath and make sure to lock the door while you're doing it."

"Don't worry, I wasn't planning on leaving anything unlocked. Especially while I'm in a bath," said Fina wryly. She cocked her head to one side. "What are you up to, Ruby Dove?"

"I need to inspect one more thing before we face the crowd downstairs. It's the last loose end. If anyone asks you where I am, just say I was having trouble with the other bath so I'm waiting for yours."

Fina nodded and padded off toward the end of the corridor. The door made a satisfying clunk noise as she locked it.

RUBY TIGHTENED the belt on her dressing gown and tiptoed down the back staircase in her bare feet. On the ground floor, she lay her body flat against the wall and crept, inch by inch, toward the drawing room. She heard the murmur of sporadic conversation.

Patting her bulging pocket, she crept closer to the staircase down to the cellar. When she had moved as close to it as possible without being seen, she removed an orange from the pocket of her dressing gown. Then she wound her arm like a cricket player and hurled the orange at the windows on the opposite side of the room.

Thud.

"What was that?" asked Adriana, jumping up from the sofa. She ran to the window. Soon everyone had moved toward the window. Ruby glided along the last few remaining steps to the cellar staircase.

She held her hand over her own mouth to prevent herself from coughing in the dusty, dank air of the cellar. Removing a candle and a book of matches from her other pocket, she tried to strike a light. After several failed attempts, she scraped her one remaining match against the stone wall. Success!

The candle flickered. Ruby held her hand around it as if she were guiding a small child through a crowd of people. Slipping softly down the steps, she made her way to the corner of the cellar containing various pieces of equipment covered in canvas. She studiously avoided looking at the wine vat.

The scraping of chairs from above told her she must hurry. Balancing the candle atop a rickety shelf, she freed her hands and lifted up the dirty, dusty canvas.

Equipment did indeed reveal itself from under the canvas. But so did something else. Canvases of another kind. Painted canvases. These were not Adriana's. Or were they? She recognised the style of Van Gogh and Monet.

Trembling, Ruby grabbed the candle from the shelf. The quick movement blew out the candle. Ruby cursed in the darkness and ran toward the stairs.

33

Clean and refreshed after their baths, but still woozy, Ruby and Fina made their way downstairs to a captive audience scattered about the drawing room. No one was looking at one another. Various inanimate objects held their attention.

Ruby settled herself into a plush green sofa as if she had become an old woman. She winced as she sat down. Fina sat next to her. It seemed the easiest course of action as she didn't have any brain power left to decide where to sit. Besides, the murderer was dead. Surely no need to be strategic.

As if all the objects around the room simultaneously became uninteresting, all eyes were on Ruby and Fina.

Ruby coughed. She smiled at Pixley who sat in a chair next to her.

"Thank you, everyone, for your patience while Fina and I tended to our needs. There was no rush, since the murderer is dead."

Fina's eyes scanned the room, noting who was missing.

Nicola.

"Where's Nicola?" asked Zenash, wringing her hands.

Fina gazed at Gina. But her glassy eyes were rimmed red.

"I know he rose during the night to go downstairs. He said he needed water," said Gina, glaring at Zenash.

Pixley twirled his spectacles. Ruby nodded at him.

"I'm afraid your husband is dead, Mrs Scarpa," said Pixley.

Gina lunged at Pixley. "You murderer!" she screamed. Renzo and Zenash rushed over to Pixley and grabbed Gina's hands before she could scratch his face.

Pixley sat down shakily in a nearby chair, wiping his head in a rhythmic motion. Ruby rose from the sofa and was soon at his side. She put a gentle hand on his shoulder. He continued to speak. "I'm sorry for your loss, Mrs Scarpa. But I did not kill your husband," he said, moving his short legs onto the bottom rung of the chair. "Your husband chased the three of us," he said, motioning toward Ruby and Fina, "out of the villa last night. We didn't realise it was your husband – all we sensed was imminent danger. As we dashed out, I fell, but I hid from Nicola. He ignored me – he was intent on pursuing Ruby and Fina."

"We hid in the studio," said Fina. "We barricaded ourselves inside. We hoped we'd be safe."

Pixley nodded. "By the time I caught up with them, I understood the situation. And the situation was dire. Your husband found paint thinner and doused the studio in it. I could tell what was going to happen. I sneaked up behind him, just as he lit a match. As I placed him in a chokehold, he dropped the match. The studio went up in flames."

"And Ruby and I kicked down a door in the back of the studio to exit just in time," said Fina. Fina was so caught up in the story she didn't consider why Ruby hadn't joined in the telling of it.

"As Ruby and Fina were struggling out the door, I was struggling with Nicola. I'm afraid he caught fire during the struggle," Pixley said softly. His head bent down in reverence. "He did what we'd probably all do in that situation – he looked for water. But the only way he could reach the water was to jump."

A collective gasp echoed around the stucco walls of the villa.

Pixley continued. "I pulled Fina from the knoll near the studio before the flames became even stronger. And, well, the rest is what you all know."

Idris jumped up. "So it means he was the murderer. And the traitor."

Renzo shrugged. "He must have been both."

"You'd better explain, Renzo. The whole story this time," said Ruby.

He looked at Nefeli. "Go on, Nefeli. Why don't you tell the story?"

Nefeli had shrunk back into the green sofa, creating an unhealthy pallor on her face. Perhaps it was just the green reflecting against her pale skin. Fina considered Nefeli – her drinking and apparent penchant for beautiful clothes she never wore. Somehow it fitted her personality. An accountant who presented a competent, efficient exterior with secrets hidden beneath.

She rose from her seat and then awkwardly sat on the arm of the sofa.

"As you're all aware, I am an accountant. As an accountant, I have an eye for detail. Renzo asked me here to help find out who was a traitor."

"A traitor to what?" asked Pixley innocently. He was a good one at playing a fool. Must come in handy as a journalist.

Nefeli cleared her throat. "To the anti-fascist cause. When I was twelve years old, Mussolini's government ordered an invasion of Rhodes. They killed my father and I swore I would take my revenge," she said, pausing to take a shaky sip of water. "In any case, I was supposed to find out which guest was a traitor to the cause. We knew from our accounts and certain intelligence we had gathered that someone in our campaign had to be a traitor."

Idris jumped up again. "But that's precisely why Renzo asked me here!"

Zenash popped up as well, as if they were playing a children's game. "Me too!"

Fina scanned the rest of the crowd. Ruggero shifted in his seat and cracked his knuckles. Fabrizio tapped his feet. Adriana's head rested on the sofa, so Fina couldn't see her expression. Gina sat still but appeared to be in her own world.

Renzo stared at the floor.

"Would you like to explain yourself, Renzo?" asked Ruby.

34

———

"Very well," he said, still staring at his shoes. They were magnificent, so it was difficult to blame him. "I believe all of you are aware we have a certain plan to carry out. Everything has become increasingly dangerous to discuss. That's one reason I decided to live on this island with Adriana. Sardinia is a hotbed of nationalism and therefore anti-fascist sentiment. That's why Nicola and I got along so well."

"But you first met Gina, didn't you?" asked Ruby.

Renzo's eyes widened. "Yes, but how did you know?"

"I suspected as much early on," said Ruby. I realised by your physique and carriage that you had been a dancer. It seemed unlikely that we'd have two dancers by coincidence."

Renzo's jaw dropped.

Ruby looked sheepish. "If I'm honest though, I researched your background before we travelled from London."

His mouth closed. Gina nodded but said nothing.

"I invited you all here under the auspices of planning that certain event. While it wasn't entirely untrue, it wasn't the full truth. I knew there was a traitor, so I told each of you I was searching for a traitor, hoping you'd do your own sleuthing or expose a secret," he said.

"Not a particularly good way to build trust, was it?" said Ruby.

Renzo's mane moved in agreement as he held out his hands. "But what choice did I have? We had to find out, otherwise the entire operation would be off," he said.

Adriana lifted her head as if she were coming out of a trance. "You'd better let me explain."

Ruby smiled.

"Renzo is taking the blame for everything, but I was the one who planned this event. It was convenient for you all to believe Renzo was at the centre of planning. It was perfectly natural for you all to assume a man would be the one leading this cause," Adriana sighed. "And it worked. All too well. I became afraid for him, especially after he became entangled with that wretched woman."

At the words "wretched woman" Gina sprung to life. "She had her claws into my husband," she spat out. "That creature couldn't just leave it at one man. No, she had to have three."

Pixley blinked.

Ruby said, "Carlotta's husband, Renzo and Nicola."

"Nicola couldn't ..." Fina trailed off as Gina shot daggers at her.

Adriana waved this tangent aside. "I worried Renzo's affair with Carlotta would jeopardise everything. Carlotta was helping to fund the project, and as someone close to the fascist regime – through her husband – she was also an ideal person to provide inside information. And Idris, Nefeli and Zenash were all important players in this scheme as well, but we had individual suspicions about them all."

"Such as?" challenged Idris.

"Your father. During the last war between Italy and Libya,

your father's side of the family agreed to support the Italians, before their real intentions became clear. But few people know that. We had suspicions you might work for the fascists, given your family history."

IDRIS SAT BACK and crossed his arms. "What you say is true about my father's side of the family, but I wouldn't let that jeopardise something as important as this plan. My family in Libya is depending on it working. Avenging my father would only bring harm to my family currently living under the Italian regime."

"And what about myself?" said Zenash, calmly folding her hands in her lap, even though her left hand trembled.

"My dear, you had at least two good reasons," said Adriana with a crooked smile.

"Oh, pish. Absolute rubbish."

"Come now. This isn't the time for games. First, while we don't question your loyalty to the anti-fascists, we pondered whether you might hesitate to go through with the plan at a critical moment. After all, most of your family is still in Ethiopia, and if you were named as a part of the plot, your family would undoubtedly suffer dreadfully. It would be only natural for you to bend under that kind of pressure."

"This is too important for me to do that," said Zenash cautiously. "My family is in trouble one way or another," she said, suddenly straightening up. "Besides, I wouldn't do anything to harm the cause – I would simply disassociate myself with it."

"I agree you might be a traitor in that way, but it wouldn't have been enough to kill Carlotta,' said Adriana. "But you had an even better non-political reason to kill her. Love. Or should I say, jealousy."

Ruby put a hand on Zenash's shoulder. "We all know, Zenash. No point in denying it."

Zenash glanced away. When she turned back, her eyes were wet. "It's true I was jealous, but it was all over with Renzo. If it weren't Carlotta, it would be someone else," she said. Suddenly her eyes lit up as she turned to Renzo. "Isn't that right, dear Renzo?"

Renzo's face was as pale as sour milk. "I don't want to discuss it, please. It's not important," he trailed off.

Fina held her head in her hands. "I'm having difficulty tracking these affairs. I thought Silvio and Ruggero overheard Renzo and Gina speaking about their own affair in the garden."

Renzo appeared sincerely puzzled. He looked at Gina, but she seemed to be in another world. "We spoke about her being together with Nicola. That he would eventually stop his affairs." He paused. "Gina?"

With pursed lips, she nodded her agreement.

"So Renzo and Gina were not having an affair," said Fina. "Silvio and Ruggero misunderstood the conversation."

"Precisely," said Renzo.

Nefeli stood up and began to pace, arms crossed. She nearly bumped into Ruby as she, too, paced in the same area. As the two women moved past each other as if they were involved in some holy ritual, Fina surveyed the room. Heads were bowed, laid back on the furniture or staring out the window. No one looked at one another.

Except Nefeli and Ruby. They had begun a staring contest. With a sudden jerk of her head, Ruby blinked and crossed her arms. She said, "Nefeli, you also had a reason to kill Carlotta, didn't you?"

Nefeli's posture became even more rigid as she continued to stare at Ruby. "Rubbish. Tommyrot, as you English say."

35

"The afternoon we arrived, Fabrizio accidentally put your suit-case in Fina's room. We inspected it to figure out who might be the owner," she said, ignoring Nefeli's sounds of spluttering. "A note fell out of the suitcase which was addressed to Carlotta. It was a threatening note that someone knew all about what she had done and that she would pay for it. It was signed 'v'."

"Visconti?" asked Idris.

"That's what Fina and I believed at first. Or 'Vito'. But I realised later the lower-case letter for 'n' in Greek is 'v', which meant it could be Nefeli. I also realised I had read the note as a figurative threat. But what if 'you will pay' was literal?" she said, staring at Nefeli with a steady gaze.

Nefeli threw her hands up in the air. "Yes, yes. I found out Carlotta was not giving us the money she had promised. In fact, she was fiddling the accounts so she could steal money from our campaign," she said, looking away from Renzo.

"What? Why didn't you tell me?" yelled Renzo.

Matching his volume in quietness, Nefeli responded, "If I had told you, you wouldn't have believed me – either when she was alive or dead. You were too in love with her. I was afraid you'd believe I was using her as a convenient excuse to cover my own pilfering of the accounts."

"Well, did you embezzle money?" asked Adriana in a quiet voice with a dangerous edge.

"No, of course not," said Nefeli, her tone changing from apologetic to angry.

Renzo marched over to Nefeli and leant over her from the back of the sofa. "If you are lying, I swear I'll ..." he trailed off.

Adriana's eyes flashed at Renzo. "It will be your fault if she did! You were so taken with Carlotta that anyone could have taken money right from under your nose."

Crack.

Ruggero's knuckle cracking had increased. It had become unbearably loud. Fina peered at Ruggero and Fabrizio. What was their role in all of this? Ruggero was so awkward. Scarcely valet material for someone so wealthy. And Fabrizio.

Fina had to intervene. She couldn't help herself. "What about Fabrizio and Ruggero? They must play a role."

Ruby said, "Why did you hire Ruggero in the first place, Renzo?"

Ruggero looked pleadingly at Renzo. Renzo coughed. "I suppose I pitied him. He had been released from military service for a host of problems. He couldn't go back to his village because it had become a sort of headquarters for the fascists in the Italian countryside. I decided we needed someone to help out, and this job provided room and board for him. He is a thorough anti-fascist to his core. He told me about what happened to his mother and father. They were early victims of the Blackshirts."

"Good lord," hissed Pixley.

Ruby removed a small notebook from her pocket. It appeared to be the one Ruggero had dropped in the corridor near their bedrooms.

"That rings true," said Ruby, biting her lip. "But there's more to this story than that, isn't there, Ruggero?" she said, handing him the notebook.

With a quivering hand, Ruggero took the clearly unwanted gift. His fingers flipped the pages, but he kept his gaze steady at the crowd.

"How did you know?" he whispered.

Renzo and Adriana shot a look of surprise and worry at Ruby.

"I was suspicious when I read the date on the first and only entry. You were using the fascist dating system of Roman numerals. 1935 is XIII since they started the new calendar beginning in 1922 with the march on Rome in 1922. At first, I thought you did it to protect yourself. But then I considered the possibility you were working for the Blackshirts. Are you working for them?"

A light breeze ruffled Ruggero's hair. But that was the only movement in the room.

"I can explain," he sighed.

"You'd better explain before I kill you myself," said Renzo, who crept toward Ruggero with his hands raised. Adriana halted his progress by leaping in front of him.

"Let him explain, Renzo. He's not going anywhere for the moment," she declared.

"When the fascists imprisoned my parents – who died a year later because of harsh treatment – I swore revenge. The local officials had the nerve to offer me a great deal of money to work for them. Can you believe their audacity? I would have spat in their face, had it not been for my younger brother and sister. The officials' offer was underlined with a not-so-subtle threat against my family if I decided not to cooperate. I agreed to their terms," he said, cracking his knuckles.

"May I have a glass of water?" asked Ruggero. "My throat is so dry I can barely speak."

Renzo's murderous face followed Adriana as she fetched water from a nearby jug.

Ruggero gulped the glass down and then wiped his brow with the back of his hand.

"Go on," growled Renzo.

Ruggero gave him a weak smile. "I was to meet Renzo and Adriana and tell them my story – which was absolutely true – and figure out a way to work for them. Though they are hard as nails, when it comes to the cause they are actually soft-hearted. They took me in and trusted me."

"Yes we did, you lying, traitorous swine," hissed Renzo.

Ruggero held up a hand. "But I haven't finished my story. When I was first employed by Adriana and Renzo, I wasn't sure if I would report their activities or not. I was so fearful for my family that I didn't know what to do. But gradually over time, I realised not only how kind they were, but the justness of their cause. I resolved I could have my revenge in a subtler way – by providing false information at key points to the Blackshirts. I would report things which didn't matter at all but then would offer a bit of information which would send them in the wrong direction. My luck would eventually run out, but what else could I do?"

"So you're saying you just pretended to work for the Black-shirts," said Pixley, chewing on the arm of his glasses.

Ruggero nodded. "And to prove it to you all, I will say what-ever you want me to when the police arrive."

Renzo now sat slumped on the sofa, head in hands. Adriana's lips were set in a grim line of understanding. Adriana held up her hand toward Fabrizio and said, "You ought to explain your-self too."

Fina took a gamble. "You're hiding something too. Why else would you pretend not to understand English?"

36

Fabrizio plopped down into a nearby chair. He spread his arms over the back and let them dangle. Fina knew about this gesture. Ruby's brother had told her this was a technique to make oneself appear bigger and more threatening. She supposed he did so unconsciously.

"You're American, aren't you, Fabrizio?" asked Ruby. "Your parents were probably from Italy or Sardinia, though."

He glanced at Adriana. She smiled at him. "Go on, tell them," she said as if she were encouraging a small child to get up on stage for their first performance.

"All right," he said, sitting up straight. His voice had taken on a different tone. Much clearer now. No wonder. "Yes, my parents were from the old country. I was born in Naples, but we moved to New York when I was a baby. My parents were deeply conservative, but I joined an anarchist syndicate when I was young. There's a network of anarchists between New York, Toronto and Detroit. Mostly they are immigrants coming from Italy, but I was one of the lucky ones – or unlucky, depending on how you look at it – who returned."

"But why were you hiding that you were American?" asked Nefeli.

"I can answer that," said Adriana. "We didn't want to arouse suspicion with the authorities in Sardinia. They're watching for these Americans who are travelling back and forth. Besides, an American will draw plenty of unwanted attention in town. No point in giving anyone a reason to pay more attention to us than was necessary."

"That solves that mystery," said Ruby. "Although Fabrizio would still have the same motive to murder the other guests – to eliminate a traitor."

Fabrizio appeared wholly unconcerned by this remark. He studied his nails.

"Wait," said Fina, gazing at Fabrizio. "Why did you have a bloody handkerchief? And those bruises on your neck?"

Fabrizio laughed. It was a bitter laugh, one borne of suffering. "I have haemophilia. It means I get nosebleeds and have strange bruises all over."

"And that must be why you refused Fina's offer of aspirin," said Ruby.

He nodded. "I wasn't hiding it from you, exactly, but I couldn't explain it to you in English because it was too complicated. And then you would have certainly figured out I was American."

"Wait a minute, Ruby," said Zenash, seemingly coming out of a trance. "Didn't we establish that Nicola was the murderer? Why would he try to kill the two of you?"

"Why indeed?" asked Ruby.

By now, Fina was accustomed to noticing that stance. The stance of the reveal. Ruby still appeared magnificent when she prepared to tell all, even if she was a little haggard from last night's adventures.

"Nicola was not the murderer," she said.

Without scanning the room, Fina sensed everyone's bodies tightening.

"But that's preposterous," exclaimed Idris. "He clearly wanted to kill you."

"What if someone led him astray? Or what if he were protecting someone?" Ruby paused. Everyone stared at Gina. "Nicola not only had an intimate relationship with his wife, obviously, but he also had one with Carlotta."

"Was there anyone Carlotta was not having an affair with?" asked Pixley.

"It would be better to ask that of Nicola, not just Carlotta," said Ruby. "Isn't that so, Zenash?"

Zenash's hands rested on each of her legs. Fina noticed Zenash's nails digging into her thigh. She flung her head back. "So what? I'm not ashamed. Yes, I had a fling with Nicola. He told me that he and Gina were essentially separated. They had both agreed to 'live and let live', as they say. I knew nothing about Carlotta."

Gina lunged at Zenash. "*Baldracca!* Strumpet!" Despite his girth, Fabrizio nimbly extricated her from Zenash within seconds.

Zenash resumed her upright posture and stroked a wisp of hair back from her face. "I did not know about Carlotta, so I had no motive to kill her. And as for poor Irene, I have no connection whatsoever. If I had wanted Nicola for myself – which I didn't – I would have killed Gina. But again, there would have been no point to that since Nicola told me they were partially estranged."

Sipping a glass of water offered by Renzo, Ruby continued. "Renzo, do you agree Nicola was a fanatic?"

Renzo nodded. "He was more dedicated to the cause than anyone I knew. If he had realised someone was a traitor, he would have had no hesitation to kill them."

"So again," said Ruby, "we're left with the fact someone told Nicola that Fina and I were traitors."

Each person in the room stared at the person next to them. Shoulders shrugged. Fina sensed Ruby was offering someone the opportunity to confess. But they remained quiet.

Cutting through the silence after a few minutes, Adriana said, "If we leave that aside for a moment, why would anyone want to kill Irene? She was such a gentle soul."

"Irene must have found out something. She was keeping a secret, too, wasn't she, Adriana?"

"What secret?" asked Pixley.

"Paintings," said Ruby.

Renzo shot a worried look at Adriana. Adriana waved aside his unspoken warning. "I'd better tell you. The reason Irene and I were somewhat secretive was not because of the nature of our relationship," she paused, licking her lips. "It was because we had an unconventional way of funding our plan. I am a painter. Irene detects forgeries and is an art expert. But the detection of forgeries works two ways, if you will. You not only detect fake paintings, but you also know how to guide someone in forging a painting correctly. That's why we had to be somewhat mysterious."

"Is that why she was in the cellar when she was killed?" asked Fina.

"It is where we kept the forgeries, but I don't know why she would suddenly go down to the cellar in the middle of dinner."

"She must have been going to meet the murderer," said Ruby.

37

"Gina," said Ruby.

Gina's head rose. She bristled like a weasel. Pixley laid a calming hand on her arm.

"You've been having headaches lately, haven't you? Severe headaches?" asked Ruby. Fina suddenly remembered Gina had mentioned them at dinner.

Gina nodded.

"And Silvio is well known for his treatments, isn't he? Not only was he treating Renzo, but he was also treating Carlotta. We found evidence of that in her room. He must have given you medicine as well."

All eyes slid toward Silvio. He lifted his interlaced hands as if to explain. "It's true. I gave her medicine."

"What was your diagnosis, Dr Rametti?" asked Ruby.

He shifted in his seat. "Well, I suppose it doesn't matter now. I believe Gina is in the early stages of a rare, degenerative nerve condition. It's almost certain to be terminal. One effect is that it becomes difficult for the victim to see things in proportion." He paused. "Isn't that true, Gina?"

Gina nodded.

"At first I took you for a jealous wife," said Ruby. "The kind of spouse who sees infidelity in the smallest gesture. But the more I learned, the more I realised you were justified in your suspicions. I expect Carlotta and Zenash were not the first lovers he had."

"No," said Gina. "He had many at a time. He always said he'd stop. He always said it was in my head. I knew it wasn't. Except then I did contract this disease, and it not only made things worse, but it gave him even more of an excuse to pretend everything was my imagination."

She rotated the small handkerchief around as if it were a rosary. "I knew about Zenash. But she had enough sense not to carry on underneath my nose."

Zenash sniffed.

"But when Carlotta breezed in, she pounced on him as if he were a tasty treat. Right in front of me that night at the pool. I couldn't take it. I didn't plan anything. I acted in the moment. And I'm not sorry."

"Then Irene began to act suspiciously. I had been poking around in the cellar and in the artist's studio. Mostly because I was searching for a place to hide the stiletto. Irene became suspicious of me. I realised that, after she pretended to twist her ankle that day. She did it to create a scene of diversion. Little did I know she was worried I would discover the forgeries. And I was worried she knew about the murder. So I arranged to meet her in the cellar during dinner. I told her it was the only time our absence wouldn't be noticed."

"Why did you stick the yellow handkerchief in her mouth?" asked Silvio.

"Nicola told me he thought Renzo invited us here to sniff out a traitor this weekend. And he was right. I hoped everyone would consider it to be a political murder – not one about infidelity. It was a rather nice touch."

Silence.

"How did you convince Nicola to try to kill us?" asked Fina.

"It wasn't too difficult after everyone was convinced the crime was about the traitor. Such a fanatic about the cause would kill quite easily. And I realised that if he were discovered, then he would be executed or thrown in jail for years. And that was fine by me. Bastard. I told him you two were the traitors, not Irene. He was so incensed and emotional about Irene's accidental death – coupled with his distress about Carlotta's murder – that he took little persuading."

Gina twisted the ring on her finger. "You must think I'm a monster. And maybe I am. But Nicola was no sweetheart, either. He not only lied and cheated behind my back, but he became downright mean when he had finished an affair with a woman," she said, turning to glare at Zenash. "Consider yourself lucky you didn't get to that point, dear."

A look of fury flashed across Zenash's face. "I'm not your dear, Gina," she said in a calm but dangerous voice. She began to rise out of her seat, but Nefeli put a hand on her shoulder.

Unperturbed by Zenash, Gina continued. "Well, what are you all going to do with me now? Turn me in?"

Fina's stomach twisted and turned. She hadn't fully considered the ramifications of solving this crime until now. What could they do?

As if in answer to her own question, Gina said with a crooked smile, "Surely you'll have to turn yourselves in if you don't turn me in."

Gina's whole body jerked, as if she were possessed by some spirit. She began to burble incoherently. Then her arms began to flail.

Nefeli leapt up latched on to one side of Gina. She nodded at Pixley to take the other. Renzo stood and held up a key, motioning to the pair to follow him upstairs.

Adriana curled into a little ball on the sofa, but still spoke. "What *are* we going to do? If the local police cannot solve this crime quickly, the Blackshirts will get involved immediately and we'll all go to jail."

"Even if we had a tidy solution, we'd still attract Blackshirt attention because of Carlotta's death," said Ruby with a sigh.

"That's correct," said Renzo as he returned down the stairs, with Nefeli and Pixley in tow. "We're all looking at jail time – best case scenario."

"Is she comfortable?" asked Ruby. Others around the room appeared scandalised by the question.

Nefeli nodded. "We locked her into her room and gave her two sleeping pills. But we were careful to not leave the bottle. Just in case."

"She seemed peaceful when we left her," said Pixley. "The room was dark, lit only by the light of those lovely pink flowers."

Adriana's head popped up. "Did you say pink flowers?"

"I didn't notice any pink flowers," said Renzo, tensing all over.

"You were attending to the sleeping tablets in the bathroom, so perhaps you didn't notice," said Pixley. "Why, is it important?"

A flash of white linen rushed across the room. Adriana flew up the stairs. Fina and Ruby were close behind. Adriana's hands were shaking so much she couldn't put the key in the lock. Ruby put a calming hand over hers and they opened the door together.

Except it wouldn't budge.

"Gina," yelled Adriana. "Let us in. Please!"

"Leave me in peace. I will not bother you anymore."

"No!" replied Ruby. "Please, please. I have something important to tell you."

Silence.

Then Fina heard shuffling and scraping. The door opened. The room was preternaturally quiet, save the clacking of a wooden blind from a half-open window in the corner.

Gina sat back down on the bed and stared at Ruby.

Adriana gasped. "Water dropwart. Sardinia is full of poisonous plants. Who picked these flowers?" she said, pointing to a sparse flower arrangement on the bedside table, next to dropped petals and a glass of water.

By now, everyone had crowded into the small room. Zenash cleared her throat. "I saw Irene picking masses of them earlier. She said she enjoyed the way the white flowers looked with their geometrical shapes – unconventional for a flower decoration with the pink flowers. Those paper-thin pink flowers are all over the island. I've been putting them in my hair for decoration."

"How did they end up in here?" asked Renzo.

Zenash said, "Nicola. He said he admired the arrangement. Irene said she would gladly give it to him as she had plenty." Her eyes widened. "You don't think he ..."

Gina was unwilling or unable to speak. She continued to stare at Ruby.

"Were you going to eat the dropwart and the oleander?" asked Renzo, bending down on his knees near Gina. She nodded. Renzo glanced up at the rest of the crowd, most of whom were standing near the doorway or in the hall by now. "The oleander are those pink flowers. Both plants are toxic. Supposedly, Sardinians used to feed the flower to ill old people and they would die with a grin on their face."

Ruby wiped her brow and plopped down on the bed. She put a hand on Gina's back. "I'm so sorry, Gina," she said, first looking at Gina and then gratefully at Adriana. "I had to go through with that charade with you downstairs because there were pieces to the puzzle that I needed you to clear up. I also wanted to see how the real murderer would react to your revelations."

Fina leant back against the door frame. "You mean Nicola and Gina aren't the murderers?"

38

A scuffling noise echoed through the corridor.

"Catch him!" yelled Ruby from inside the room.

Fabrizio, Ruggero and Silvio locked arms in the corridor, shoving one another. The trio began to wrestle, though Fina couldn't tell who was holding who back.

"Oof," she groaned, as Fabrizio's fist accidentally punched her in the gut. She doubled over. As she slid to the floor, clutching her stomach, she saw Ruggero's face contorted in agony, while Fabrizio's became nearly unrecognisable through his wrinkled, bulldog-like countenance. She couldn't see Silvio's face as his back was toward her, but she could see his hair shaking.

A sudden yelp broke up the trio's locked embrace.

Fabrizio had grabbed Silvio's hair.

"*Lasciami*! Let me go!" he screeched.

Ruby's head popped out of the doorway. "Where did you think you'd escape to, Dr Rametti?"

"Silvio?" cried Renzo. "You mean he is the murderer? Impossible. He's a doctor. He heals people." Adriana held Renzo tightly, as if he were a small child about to wriggle out of her arms.

Silvio sat up but remained on the floor as Fabrizio stood blocking the exit to the stairs. The crowd of guests blocked the only other exit. He ran his hands through his hair. It was no longer the picture of his controlling and calm personality.

"Are you injured, Fina?" asked Ruby, rushing toward her.

"I'm fine, thanks," said Fina, rising to her feet. "I want to know what happened."

Ruby, smiled, nodded and leant against the opposite doorway. "We realised these murders could not be solved by examining everyone's alibis. After all, everyone had the opportunity to kill Carlotta and Irene. And motives were scarcely in short supply for at least one, if not two, of the victims."

"So what remains?" asked Idris.

"Psychology, as well as the psychology behind the way they were killed," answered Ruby, smoothing her hair. Though she was playing the part well, Fina could tell by her slightly drooping posture that Ruby was exhausted. And no wonder. This sleuthing and spying business was not easy.

"We've established the people with distressed psychologies, such as Renzo, Carlotta, Gina, and perhaps Nicola, were not the murderers. So why Dr Rametti?" asked Zenash.

"I first had to ask myself why Carlotta was drowned in the pool. And second, why Irene was drowned in the vat with the additional clue of the yellow handkerchief. If we take Irene's murder first, we can see that whoever set it up either wanted to send a message to the traitor or wanted to implicate someone in the crime via political means. Either way, it would look like Irene was the traitor."

"But she wasn't the traitor!" cried Adriana.

"I know, Adriana. I'm just explaining my thought process. Carlotta's murder appeared to be either personal or political.

But I had to ask myself why she was drowned and then stabbed, or stabbed and then drowned. I couldn't fathom it. Why go to all that trouble? Moreover, why wouldn't you just pitch her body into the sea? Then there wouldn't be any chance of us investigating what happened."

"Do you mean Silvio wanted the body to be found?" asked Fina.

"Precisely. What we had in both crimes was an attempt to frame someone else. I'm not saying there weren't individual motives to kill both, but there was something larger at work here. When Fina and I ascertained Silvio had lied about the knife we found being the knife which killed Carlotta – we, or at least I, thought he lied because he was afraid it might be Adriana or Renzo's letter opener. In other words, he convinced us, implicitly, that he was lying to protect Renzo and Adriana, either of whom could have been murderers," said Ruby.

"But you're saying now it was exactly the opposite," said Zenash.

"I racked my brains as to why someone would not only drown her in the pool but also stab her. And then it came to me," Ruby said. "Could someone fetch me a glass of water?"

Fina smiled. Even though she was tired, Ruby would not lose the chance to savour this moment.

Idris returned from Gina's room with a glass of water.

Thirst satiated, Ruby carried on. "We noticed a possible pathway in the shrubbery through which the body had been dragged, so it seemed plausible she was stabbed and then thrown in the pool. She also had other signs that she was killed rather than drowned. But again, why go to all that trouble? Besides, there was a great risk it would accidentally create a great splash in the pool which would wake everyone in the house."

"Is it because there was something Silvio needed to hide about her dying before she was thrown in the pool?" asked Fina

"Bingo! I thought it had to do with the stabbing. But then I realised it was a diversion. And we had all fallen for the diversion. The diversion was for us to obsessively puzzle about why she needed to be attacked twice in these different ways," said Ruby. "It was to divert us from the actual way she was murdered."

"Yes, go on, dammit," growled Renzo, who was now in tears.

"What if she were poisoned? Now, anyone could have poisoned her, just as they could have stabbed or drowned her. But why would the murderer want to cover up a poisoning?"

"Because suspicion in a poisoning would naturally fall on a doctor," said Idris, flashing a smile of triumph at Fina. "Especially one who hands out medicinal options as if they were candy."

Silvio groaned and held his head. "Yes, yes. I considered it the best way. You would be diverted by all the red herrings, as they call them in detective stories – politics, jealousy, money and revenge. If I tried to murder Carlotta by poisoning, suspicion would naturally fall on me. At the very least I would be investigated by local Sardinian authorities."

"But it wouldn't be certain you would be convicted. After all, it could be others who had access to dangerous drugs – or even, as we've seen, flowers," said Adriana.

"I'm not certain, but I suspect it's because you couldn't take the chance of a thorough investigation by Sardinian local officials, some of whom would be well connected to the Scarpas and also be pro-Sardinian nationalists," said Ruby.

Fina was concerned that Renzo's eyes might actually fall on the floor. "Are you saying you work for the Blackshirts?" he sputtered.

39

Silvio didn't move, but the set line of his lips indicated affirmation. Then words tumbled forth. "Like many others, I was seduced by and then forced to work for the Blackshirts. I proved myself a loyal follower, and soon I was able to move about without having someone follow me all the time. I also made it clear to my superiors that I couldn't be hampered by having to communicate frequently – so they don't even know I'm here this weekend."

His hands quivered as he continued. "Because of Renzo's high-profile political statements, my job was to get as close to him as possible. Of course, being a doctor was precisely the way to do that. I was trained in psychology, so it wasn't too difficult to convince Renzo that his minor ailments – mostly related to growing older – were connected to his mental state. I was so successful at this that I tried the same with Gina and Carlotta."

"But why did Carlotta need to die? And poor Irene?" asked Adriana.

"Because Carlotta had become a liability, as they say. Her behaviour was becoming more and more erratic. It seemed like she betrayed Renzo, but then she would suddenly and capriciously change her mind and pass information to other anti-fascists. And Irene. That was sad. But she knew too much. She didn't know who committed the murder, but she made Gina nervous enough that she told me about her suspicions."

"But wait a moment," said Pixley. "Gina admitted to these crimes. Why did she do that?"

"I'm afraid the power of suggestion and gentle hypnosis can convince someone like Gina she had committed the crime," said Silvio.

Fina realised that must be the reason for the note directing Gina to speak to Silvio. It had nothing to do with an affair.

"Oh, it was much more than that, Dr Rametti," said Ruby. "Fina and I figured out that both Carlotta and Gina were taking a drug called Ergoapiol for various female issues. This drug is only given under a physician's supervision. I had difficulty remembering why the drug was significant. I tried to recall my chemistry lectures. And then I realised the reason this drug is so memorable is that a common side effect is hallucinations. The drug is made from a fungus which grows on rye. It has been in use for centuries, but the side effects can be extreme."

"But wouldn't all of this draw attention to yourself? Didn't you say you were worried about local officials investigating your background?"

Silvio grimaced.

Ruby coughed. "There's one last piece of the puzzle," she said, turning the handle on the door to Silvio's room behind her.

Everyone moved into the room while Fabrizio held Silvio in the hallway. Ruby smoothed her hand over the wallpaper near the door. "As you all know, wallpaper often peels up at one end because of moisture or has little bubbles of air trapped beneath the surface," she said, and demonstrated by peeling up the edge of a seam of the wallpaper nearest to her.

"This also means it makes an excellent hiding place if you peel back the paper and insert small objects inside."

Fina blinked. So did everyone else.

Ruby grinned. "I'd like to ask everyone's assistance in examining one section of the wall for any large bulges or bumps."

"What are we searching for?" asked Adriana.

"Just humour me. Look for any irregularities," said Ruby as she pressed her hand against the wall.

Everyone's eyes crinkled with puzzlement, but they split up around the room and went to work.

Fina and Idris slid the wardrobe away from the wall. As they did so, he touched her hand. Her fingers tingled. Their eyes met for a moment, but broke apart as Ruggero approached.

"Need help?" he asked.

"Yes," said Idris. "We need to move it out just a few more inches so we can slide behind it."

Soon the wardrobe stood at least a foot from the wall. Fina slipped in between. She ran her fingers over every inch.

"Here it is, Ruby!" she yelled, knowing the wardrobe would muffle her voice. "There's a definite bump. Should I take off the wallpaper?"

"Yes, please do," she said, handing her a pair of scissors through the gap between the wardrobe and the wall.

She drew a circle around the bulge and peeled back the paper to reveal ... a letter opener. The stiletto. Fina slid out from behind the wardrobe with her quarry.

Renzo gasped. "That's my letter opener. I keep it locked in my desk."

"Yes, I know. You must have lied when we were all together in the study and you pretended the knife was in the drawer," said Ruby.

"Ah, well, yes, I did. After Carlotta was murdered, I found it had disappeared," he said. "But I thought the murderer must have thrown it into the sea. That was the most logical explanation ... and, well, I didn't want to cast suspicion on myself," he added sheepishly.

Ruby held it aloft for everyone to see. "This was actually the knife used to stab, but not kill, Carlotta. Silvio was going to turn it into the authorities and you, Renzo, would be immediately implicated since you were somewhat fanatical about holding onto your keys. Rightly so."

"So that means Silvio would escape a thorough investigation into his background," said Nefeli, eyes glowing like a cat.

"Even if there were to be an investigation, the initial detention of Renzo under suspicion of murder would give Silvio enough time to ask his contacts in the government for additional protection," said Ruby.

"But how did you realise the stiletto was in Silvio's room, much less hidden in the wallpaper?" exclaimed Pixley. His rapidly twirling glasses had become a blur.

Fina stepped forward. The fog was beginning to lift in her mind. "The afternoon we arrived, we heard an odd scraping noise coming from Silvio's room. It was certainly an odd sound, but I didn't think much of it. Later, we found bits and pieces of what appeared to be white paper in the hallway. That, too, on its own meant little. The pieces were so small that it looked more like dust. We would have been suspicious had they been larger pieces of paper."

Ruby nodded. "Some of the tiny bits of wallpaper must have fallen onto Silvio's clothes and he might have brushed them off in the corridor. It made perfect sense once I mulled it over. It's normal for people to inspect clothing when they leave their room and ready themselves to go downstairs."

"So you're saying Silvio had two reasons for murdering Carlotta. One was to eliminate her as a 'loose cannon', I believe it's called in English, and the second was to frame Renzo, and possibly Adriana, in the process," said Nefeli.

Scuffling and screaming came from the hallway. Everyone dashed into the corridor. Fina spotted Silvio's hair, but not Silvio, descending the staircase. Fabrizio was close behind, but he slipped as he made his way down the staircase. Ruggero and Zenash rushed after to help pull up Fabrizio. As soon as they lifted him, he cried out in pain.

Fina glanced down at Fabrizio's legs. An ankle was twisted the wrong way. She winced from sympathy and squeamishness. Ruggero and Zenash held him up by each arm and they made their way slowly downstairs.

"But Silvio has escaped," cried Idris. "I will find him," he said, jaw clenched.

"But he cannot go anywhere," said Fina. Too late. Idris had already disappeared.

40

"Well, what do we do now?" asked Pixley as they all settled out on the terrace to soak up the morning sun. No one wanted to sit inside the villa.

"First, you're not going to write any of this down, Mr Hayford," said Ruby. "No journalists here."

Pixley nodded. He grasped the gravity of the situation.

The curtains hanging over the doorway to the terrace parted. Idris dragged himself in and flopped down on the nearest chair. His hair was dishevelled, and he looked utterly bewildered.

He looked up at the crowd dispersed among the furniture of the drawing room. "Silvio is dead."

"What?" demanded Renzo. "How?"

"I followed him, but I couldn't catch up with him. He's quite fit. He moved toward the burned remains of the studio, and then suddenly took a running jump off the cliff. I looked over the edge and spotted his body on the rocks. It was clear he was dead. And what was also clear is that he will be carried away with the tide, as it is low tide now," he said, shaking his head and burying it in his hands.

Fabrizio appeared with coffee and tea. Though everyone

appeared too embarrassed to accept his offer of a hot beverage at a time like this, soon everyone's countenance had improved. "Where's Gina?" asked Idris.

"She's sleeping in her room," said Adriana. "We don't have to worry about her committing suicide any longer."

Renzo gazed at his watch. "It's just about time for the ferry to arrive. Or I should say stop near the island. They know to expect our boat, so if we don't show up it will be only a few more hours before one of my friends – or the police – decide to make their way here." He ran his hands through his mane.

Ruby tapped her teeth. "We're all exhausted, but let's talk through all the possible scenarios of what can happen next. Then we can all try to sleep. If that's at all possible."

They all stared at Adriana and Renzo.

"You two have the best idea since you live locally," said Ruby. "What is likely to happen?"

Renzo's trembling hand tried to light a cigarette twice. Pixley had to intervene. Once he had taken his first inhale, his body relaxed. "The first scenario is this. The local police arrive in a few hours. We explain what happened, they detain us all and notify the national police because of Carlotta's involvement. Then the Blackshirts step in, and we all go to jail. For a long time."

Pixley's mouth dropped open. "What's the other scenario?"

Renzo shrugged. He watched Adriana. She sat back, arms behind her head holding her hair tightly back from her face. She closed her eyes in a gesture of what must have been deep contemplation.

"Let's suppose, just for a moment, the police arrive and we say we were stranded," said Zenash.

"Why would we be stranded?" asked Fina.

"Kidnapped!" exclaimed Idris. "What if Carlotta, Irene, Nicola and Silvio were kidnapped?"

Renzo goggled at him. "Sounds a little far-fetched, doesn't it?"

"It doesn't sound much more far-fetched than the actual truth," said Pixley quietly.

"Let's entertain that idea for a moment," said Ruby. "If we tell them they were kidnapped, what would happen next?"

"Again, because of Carlotta's involvement, the Blackshirts would step in and use it as an excuse to detain us indefinitely," said Adriana, opening her eyes.

"So the problem is Carlotta, and to a lesser extent, Silvio. If we take her out of the scenario for a minute, what happens?"

Adriana gave a little cough. "Well, no one is aware Irene was here. She told her friends and family she was going to Florence to consult with experts at the Uffizi Gallery. For obvious reasons, she didn't want anyone to know she was here," she said, twisting the loose folds of her clothing. "And we were close, very close. But we didn't tell anyone about that. Only Renzo knew."

"And there's nothing in her past to connect her to either Carlotta or to the Scarpas, correct?" asked Ruby.

Adriana nodded.

"So what if we said Nicola was supposed to come this weekend, but never arrived?" asked Ruby. "Separate from Gina."

"How do we explain the fact we were stranded?" asked Fina.

"What if Nicola took out the boat and never returned?" asked Pixley. "We are certain someone cut the boats loose – either Nicola, Gina or Silvio. The boats will be found somewhere, at some point, and people will believe they had a boating accident. Perhaps not the little dinghies, but most definitely Renzo's own large boat."

Renzo slapped his thigh. "That's it! That's brilliant," he said waving his cigarette around in little circles. "The police can believe that precisely because my boat will be missing from the harbour. As for the little dinghy, we can say Nicola took that with him because he didn't have one of his own."

"What about Carlotta?" asked Idris.

Ruby paced in small circles rather than her usual longer running-track circuit. She looked up at Renzo. "Does her husband know she is here? It sounds like they led mostly separate lives."

Renzo's cigarette hung out of the side of his mouth. He chewed it absently. "Carlotta was well aware of the danger of her husband finding out about us – not because of the infidelity, but because of my political associations. When we met in the past, she always told her husband she was going to visit a friend somewhere well away from Sardinia."

"We'll have to take a chance that she said she was going elsewhere," said Ruby.

Fina knew Ruby didn't have to tell this crowd to be quiet about what had happened at the villa that weekend. Everyone was well aware of the danger.

"What will you tell your boss?" asked Renzo, glancing at Ruggero. Ruggero shrugged. "That nothing of interest happened here this weekend. I will say I found out something about the Scarpas, however, to make them happy. That won't harm anyone."

"What about Silvio? How do we explain his disappearance?" asked Fina.

"There's nothing to explain," said Renzo. "As Silvio said, he was a lone wolf when working with the Blackshirts, so they don't even know he was here. I know he was estranged from his entire family. He lived the life of a hermit – his only so-called friends were his patients. If an acquaintance happened to find out he was travelling to the island, we could say he never arrived."

Scanning the room, Fina surveyed a host of limp and

exhausted bodies. But everyone's heads were nodding as slowly as if a puppeteer was pulling their strings in unison.

A loud booming sounded from somewhere offshore.

"What's that noise?" asked Pixley.

"It's the blessed ferry. Not long now before we all get off the island, thanks to the brilliant brains of one Miss Ruby Dove."

"And a thank you in advance to Mr Pixley Hayford, who will still get his scoop," said Ruby with a wan smile. "A gentleman through and through, who I'm sure we can rely on to keep certain details to himself."

The ferry boomed again in the distance.

EPILOGUE

La Nuova Terranova Pausania

Shoemaker Vanishes at Sea

A well-known couple in Terranova Pausania vanished this weekend at sea. Nicola Scarpa, owner of Scarpa shoes, and his wife, Gina, a dancer, were guests of a Mr Renzo Carnevali at his private villa on the Agrodolce Island. Mr Scarpa told Mr Carnevali he would sail to a nearby island to have lunch and return that evening. Local police found their boat washed up against the rocks near Tavolara Island, but there was no sign of Mr Scarpa. Mr Carnevali said he had been a dear friend and pillar of the local community. Mrs Scarpa could not be reached for comment. The funeral will be held this Saturday at Santa Fina Church.

Gazzetta di Sardegna

Opera Singer Missing

Carlotta Visconti, opera singer and wife of leather magnate Vito Visconti, has been missing since last Wednesday. According to her husband, she left to stay with friends in Vicenza for a long weekend. The family friends could not be reached for comment, but local police are making enquiries. Mr Visconti commented he believed anti-fascist forces were behind his wife's disappearance: "I will find these traitors and punish them accordingly," he said as he left the police office in Vicenza. Anyone who has information about the beloved opera singer should contact their local authorities.

ENJOYED RUBY'S STILETTO?

I'm looking to you, dear reader, to share your views about this series. Reviews online are wonderful and word of mouth is even better.

If you enjoyed this book, I would be grateful if you spent a few minutes leaving me a review (for any or all mysteries!) on Amazon. Nothing elaborate is needed. One a sentence is enough.

The Ruby Dove Mystery Series:
The Mystery of Ruby's Sugar
The Mystery of Ruby's Port
The Mystery of Ruby's Smoke
Box Set: Mysteries 1-3
The Mystery of Ruby's Stiletto

Join my reader group! You'll have the opportunity to join my advance reader team, get occasional goodies, and receive updates about new releases. Sign up at rosedonovan.com.

Thank you!

ABOUT THE AUTHOR

Rose Donovan is a lifelong devotee of cozy mysteries. *The Ruby Dove Mystery Series* is her first foray into fiction, though she has written numerous non-fiction articles unraveling the mysteries of politics and injustice.

www.rosedonovan.com
rose@rosedonovan.com

NOTE ABOUT BRITISH STYLE

Readers fluent in US English may believe words such as "fuelled", "signalled", "hiccough", "fulfil", titbit", "oesophagus", "blinkers", and "practise" are typographical errors in this text. Rest assured this is simply British spelling. There are also other formatting differences in terms of spacing and punctuation, including periods after quotation marks in certain circumstances. I certainly learned a lot when making sure the prose was accurate!

For Mom